W10

LOVE ADRIFT

In Haven Bay, facing a raging blizzard, lifeboatman Steve Day and his crew pick up survivors from the wrecked Channel Ferry. The blizzard isolates Haven Bay and schoolmistress Helen Foster fears for her boyfriend, a passenger on the ship. Steve Day gives her no time to despair, with a boatload of survivors to look after. But the villagers' concern and help for them is returned by havoc and danger, while Helen discovers an awakening to her way of life.

W. S. FOORD

LOVE ADRIFT

Complete and Unabridged

LINFORD
Leicester

First published in Great Britain in 1976

First Linford Edition
published 2010

British Library CIP Data

Foord, W. S.
  Love adrift. - - (Linford romance library)
  1. Lifeboat crew members- -Fiction.
  2. Search and rescue operations- -Fiction.
  3. Women teachers- -Fiction.
  4. Love stories. 5. Large type books.
  I. Title II. Series
  823.9′14–dc22

  ISBN 978–1–44480–034–0

Published by
F. A. Thorpe (Publishing)
Anstey, Leicestershire

Set by Words & Graphics Ltd.
Anstey, Leicestershire
Printed and bound in Great Britain by
T. J. International Ltd., Padstow, Cornwall

This book is printed on acid-free paper

1

The twenty-five infants at Haven Bay Primary School had never found Helen Foster to be a bad tempered schoolmistress, in fact they were in agreement that she was both nice and pretty. On this last day of term before Christmas, however, they had never known her to be so happy.

Helen was letting them go early so that they could return home and put on their best dresses before attending the school party at six p.m.

She asked them to tidy the desks before the helpers came up from the village to arrange the classroom and prepare the mammoth tea, and as the infants filed past the radiant Helen, they seemed reluctant to take their eyes off her, even if a sparkling and mysterious Christmas tree had been planted and decorated in the corner of the room to attract their attention.

'See you all at six,' Helen reminded them.

The infants, rosy faced and bright eyed beneath the paper decorations that swung across the ceiling, nodded vigorously and waved their small hands before darting out of the ancient, squat grey building to meet their mothers, waiting outside in the raw, bleak afternoon.

Helen followed the infants out of the school to satisfy herself that no pupil would have to make her own way down to the short trip of sea front that contained the isolated village of Haven Bay.

As the infants, together with their mothers dispersed, Helen stayed for a while out of doors to get a breath of fresh air.

Despite the coldness and she wore no coat, Helen strolled towards the sea front. She stopped and stood between a couple of winches, then looked out on to the heaving grey water of the Channel.

She could not fail to experience a

twinge of excitement, although she realised it was several hours too soon before the Channel Ferry left Ostend, but the fact that only twenty-two miles separated her from her loved one, gave her a sense of yearning that no patience could overcome.

She was still staring out to sea when Steve Day hailed her from the huge steel shed that housed the local lifeboat.

Helen half turned and smiled generously. Steve needed no more encouragement than that. He strode towards her in long sea boots and a short duffel coat.

He was tall, strong and cheerful, and his face never lost the dark tan from one end of the year to the other. Steve was the only full-time member of Haven Bay's lifeboat crew. Ashore he undertook the duty of lifeboat secretary and was responsible for servicing the craft, while afloat, he was first choice for the boat's coxswain.

Because the village possessed such a wonderful record for rescuing ship-wrecked seamen and giving care and comfort to wretched survivors, the lifeboat had become the most vital factor in the lives of the tiny community. Steve had launched the boat into the spiteful and narrow Straits during the past year more times than any other lifeboat around the coast, and the number of lives saved filled the hearts of the villagers with pride. It was a hard fact, that the rugged and likeable Steve was the most important man in the village, and his attraction towards the petite and attractive schoolmistress pleased everyone.

The couple worked hand in hand and gave up their leisure time to raise funds for the local lifeboat and provide amenities in the village for survivors that were brought ashore from a congested shipping lane.

Together, they organised dances and whist drives. They had put on and acted in a successful play only last month, and the village school had been packed for each of the six performances. It was necessary that they spent many hours together, and the local residents could see nothing but good coming from such an arrangement.

Steve knew he was in love with Helen. He could not wish for a better person to become his wife. They were such excellent friends. Never in serious dispute over anything, and he could not understand it when Helen was forced to tell him, that they were in fact, just good friends.

It still confused him, that Helen could produce a stranger almost out of the blue, who she declared she loved, and her feelings for Tommy Carr were different, unexplainably different to those she held for Steve.

Steve had growled his dissatisfaction at the situation for the past month, never really convinced that Helen was serious about this other character. He waited patiently, never aggressive, hoping he would still be the first to hear from Helen's lips that she had made a mistake, and that Tommy Carr could not compare with him.

Perhaps on this stormy afternoon in late December, Steve had mistaken Helen's sudden arrival on the sea front, braving the bitter wind without bothering to put on a coat, as a sign that she wanted to see him on an urgent matter.

'That's a lovely smile on a raw afternoon,' he greeted Helen.

'I always smile when I am happy,' Helen told him.

Steve towered above her. He spoke unhesitatingly:

'I guess I was hoping you had come to see me.'

'I'm pleased to see you, Steve,' admitted Helen.

He seemed suddenly aware that he had dirty hands while standing close to this spotlessly dressed young woman, and he fumbled with a piece of cotton waste from the pocket of his duffel coat and intently wiped the grease from his hands.

'Been checking the starter motor,' he explained.

'I dismissed the children early so that

they can get ready for the party — then I came for a breath of fresh air.'

'Oh — that's all?'

Helen shrugged.

'More or less. Perhaps I'm indulging in a spot of day dreaming.'

'Looking out to sea for your lover, eh!'

'Please, Steve . . . don't.'

'Why? Isn't that what you were doing?'

Helen ignored his question, and said:

'It hurts you when we discuss Tommy.'

Steve bit his lip and declared:

'I never thought when you first told me you had met Tommy Carr, that one day — it would be too late for me to do anything about it.'

He examined her eyes that were full of a candid expression and added:

'Is it really too late, Helen?'

His voice was so tender coming from such a powerful man that she felt cruel in having to tell him the truth.

'Tommy is coming across on the

Channel Ferry, this evening.'

Steve grunted and nodded in the direction of the headland, just six miles across the snug, little bay.

'Docking at Highport?' he assumed.

'I'm going to meet him after the children's party.'

'Then — what?'

'I shall stay with Tommy's family for Christmas. If they like me, I guess we'll be married in the New Year.'

Steve sighed, and kept his eyes glued to the town of Highport that was perched on the headland and jutting aggressively towards the coast of France and Belgium.

'Who could not help liking you,' muttered Steve. 'It just beats me how I missed out.'

'It has nothing to do with you, Steve. I like you and always will do, but I met Tommy . . .'

Steve laughed at himself.

'I suppose if I hadn't recommended you to the Two Cities Travel Agency in Highport, I wouldn't be standing here complaining that I have lost you to another man.'

'It did start the day I went to arrange a day trip to France for the schoolchildren, but I never expected such personal service. Tommy doubted if I could handle twenty-five pupils alone, so he came along as escort. It turned out to be a marvellous day,' concluded Helen.

Steve gave up.

'Well, in case I don't see you before Christmas — have a good time.'

Helen watched Steve retreat to the familiar refuge of the lifeboat shed where he had won such a fine reputation as being the man in charge of that valiant boat, then becoming conscious of the cold wind, she retraced her steps to the school.

Once the helpers had arrived and everyone became energetically involved in preparing the tables for the party, Helen found that it was possible to dismiss Tommy's homecoming from her mind.

He had taken out a party of tourists for a stay in Paris for the Christmas season, and after checking on a few complaints, he was returning to the headland town of Highport where his travel agency was based.

She simply prayed for his safe arrival and then entered into the spirit of the Christmas party.

Helen called a halt when the youngsters were becoming weary of the games and after each had been given a present from the sparkling tree, and a few colourful balloons had been salvaged for the children to take home, the classroom emptied, leaving Helen with a trio of helpers and a mountain of débris.

After the washing up was completed, Helen thanked her helpers and when one protested that there was an awful lot of muddle to be cleared up, Helen insisted that they had done enough and she would cope with straightening the classroom with the assistance of Judd, the caretaker.

'Thank you all very much,' said Helen, as she opened the stout timber door for them.

'See you after Christmas?'

'Of course.'

She closed the door behind them, and stood surveying the heap of fallen decorations and the tree that had shed much of the brilliance during the past hour.

She revelled in the quietness for a few minutes. It had been a splendid year. She had arrived at Haven Bay for her first appointment since finishing at the Teacher's Training College with the twin ambitions of making a success of her career and being accepted by the close knit community.

Helen felt she had succeeded. Her own ability made her a respected and popular teacher, while she owed a lot to Steve Day for making her a valuable member of the community.

She shuffled through the littered floor making furrows as she went, and collected a broom from the kitchen, but the caretaker caught her with it as he arrived.

The door was ajar and a savage wind invaded the room scattering the discarded decorations to all four corners.

'Leave that, Miss Foster. I'll see to the clearing up,' said Harry Judd.

'There is far too much . . .'

'''Tis what I'm paid to do.'

Judd had spent forty years at sea, but he was still active and upright. Nothing appeared to be too much trouble for him in his work, and it seemed incredible that he was a pensioner of almost seventy.

'But not to shift a mountain of rubbish at this time of night,' objected Helen.

'You get off home before you get caught in the snow.'

Helen raised her eyebrows.

'Is it going to snow?'

'Certain of it.'

Judd took the broom from Helen, and added wisely:

'Get some canned food in your store — just in case.'

Helen was thinking more of Tommy making the Channel crossing on a savage sea than the necessity to hoard supplies.

'I am going away for Christmas,' she announced.

'Going far?'

'Over to Highport.'

'Best get started shortly,' advised Judd.

'Is the weather going to get as bad as that, Mr. Judd?'

'When blizzards 'it the Straits and the snow lays on the cliffs beyond, the drifts are high as 'ouses,' warned Judd.

'This is my first winter here,' Helen reminded him.

'You can see the lay out o' the village yerself. Tucked all snug like in the middle o' the bay wi' only the single coastal road joining us wi' Highport over at the headland and North Foreland in t'other direction.'

'Does the road get blocked?'

'Terrible it is. 'Tis nothing for the village to be cut off for three days on end.'

Helen thought about the small community isolated from the rest of the country, and wondered what on earth they did to relieve the boredom.

'I hope your weather forecast is wrong,' said Helen, softly.

Judd sniffed and started to push on the broom.

''Taint my forecast, Miss Foster. Gales imminent in the Straits, followed by snow storms. That's what it said on the radio. Put the two together and you got yourself a blizzard.'

Helen took heed of the old man's warning. She collected her belongings, put on a coat, wished the caretaker a happy Christmas and then turned out into the bitterly cold night.

The wind from the sea, both howled and had a knife edge to it. Helen walked swiftly along to the sea front where she had lodgings in one of the old coastguard cottages. Solid, square buildings of rock and shiplap and sold off to the local residents when the modern coastguard station was built on the headland.

The cottages made ideal summer homes, and the people who had acquired them, rented off rooms for seasonal visitors, because Haven Bay was an ideal spot for fishing and boating enthusiasts.

Helen had managed to find all the year lodgings with Miss Pegler, a retired nursing sister, who was glad of Helen's permanence to help out with her small pension.

As she passed the lifeboat station, Helen observed that there was a light on in the room that Steve used as his office and nerve centre of the station.

It gave her an uncomfortable sensation when she saw too that he had flung open the huge doors of the shed, and the yawning gap faced the concrete slipway that led to the sea.

The tide was coming in fast, and Helen switched to the far side of the sea front to walk on as the frothy spray spattered against the wall. Then as she reached the cottage where she lodged, a large flurry of snow fell on her bare head.

2

Helen frowned impatiently as the mirror on her dressing table tilted and robbed her of the reflection of her hair as she tried to get it into some kind of style.

She had packed a suitcase, changed into a warm suit and was putting the finishing touches to her face when the sea thumped against the sea wall, causing the little cottage to shudder.

It was blowing up rough, and according to plan, Tommy would be aboard the Channel Ferry by now.

Helen had the place to herself. Miss Pegler, who had suffered from blizzards in the past and once gone hungry when the village was cut off for a week and the shops had sold out of food, had taken stock of her larder and ignoring the spiteful weather gone along to the corner shop to fill her shopping basket with tinned foods in case of an emergency.

She straightened the mirror and quickly swept her hair back off her forehead, then put on some stout walking shoes, and inspected her watch.

The bus that called at the village en route to Highport was due in ten minutes. She wasn't sure if her watch was correct, so she switched on her transistor to check the time.

A weather forecast was being read in advance of the eight p.m. news bulletin, and it made uneasy listening.

The Straits were pinpointed as the location for gales — force eight, accompanied by snow.

'Phew — eighty mile an hour winds,' mused Helen.

She grew anxious. The Channel Ferry would have to fight like a tiger to meet the challenge of the roaring and savage sea.

It did not matter that there was only twenty-two miles of water to cross, and that the ship was fitted with radar and manned by an efficient crew. Waiting for Tommy was becoming an ordeal!

Helen crossed the room and picked up her case, turned out the light and nipped downstairs. She scribbled a short note to Miss Pegler, then ventured out of doors.

The snow was laying and the sea front glistened with the smooth whiteness. She gripped her case and plodded along the front to meet the bus.

Then she froze, not with the severity of the bitter night, but a loud explosion erupted from the lifeboat station, and a rocket tore into the sky leaving an amber trail in its wake.

Helen stood still as if it was an outrage to move while the volunteer members of the lifeboat crew were summoned to duty.

She heard a door open and a man's voice sounded crisp and dry:

'The maroon's gone up!'

She seemed to become lost in the activity that followed and men trudged past her, leaving her as if she was a statue.

Helen was no stranger to the lifeboat drill. From the first day she had become involved with Steve, her heart had ached when the lifeboat was called out. The message flashed from the coastguard on watch at the headland station to Steve on duty in the lifeboat station.

He would fire the rocket that called the volunteers to launch the boat.

Then, the proud craft slid down the slipway into the surf, the twin propellors churned the water as the lifeboat plunged into the waves that beat against the sea wall.

Then out to the open and lonely sea to answer the distress call. It all happened like that tonight. Helen watched the oilskin clad figures working the ropes and tackle as the lifeboat charged into the attack on the unruly sea, and peering through the thick snow she tried to identify Steve.

For the moment, she forgot about the

bus she wanted to meet, and she closed her eyes tightly and prayed:

'God — have mercy on poor souls out on such a night.'

When she opened her eyes, the lifeboat was safely launched, and quickly became lost from view under the high seas and frantic snowstorm.

She remembered weakening once, when Steve was called out, daring to suggest that she wished he didn't have to go. It was the only occasion when he had been really curt with her.

'The lifeboat is my job and my life. I'm paid for saving souls . . . spare your thoughts to the volunteers who come forward and don't count the cost.'

Helen never mentioned the risk involved again, but that didn't say she stopped worrying.

A cluster of villagers braved the elements for a while to watch from the shore, but the fury of the blizzard sent them back indoors where they kept up a vigil behind parted curtains.

The Haven Bay lifeboat was modern,

considered unsinkable and fitted with radar and modern radio communications, but the locals kept up the tradition of watching and waiting.

Helen came out of her dazed state and advanced to the end of the sea front. She turned towards the High Street, and avoided the queue that spilled on to the pavement outside the corner shop, where the owner had kept open late to supply the prudent villagers with emergency rations.

She stopped at the bus stop. The village was a curious mixture of Christmas lights in shop windows, heavily falling snow, a dark sea front with high seas pounding the wall, and the local lifeboat thrashing through the fiery Channel.

She watched a police Panda car skim past, blue light flashing, and caught a glimpse of the village constable. He shouted out to Helen, but she lost the words in the wind, and she never knew if it was a greeting or what.

The Panda was swiftly followed by

Jim Marsh, the young doctor who shared the village practice with his more experienced father. Jim was behind the wheel of his big station wagon, and looked grim and determined. He gestured to Helen with a helpless shrug of his shoulders, but never reduced speed as he headed towards Foreland Hill.

Helen waited on, but the bus never came. She was growing wet and cold. She thought about Mr. Judd's warning that if she didn't get out of the village to Highport immediately, the blizzard would close in and the drifts block the coastal road.

She imagined Tommy's disappointment when he stepped ashore and found she was not waiting for him. She had promised and she wasn't going to allow a blizzard to rob her of that warm embrace that Tommy greeted her with when they met.

She stuck by the bus stop until a man approached her, who had walked two miles down Foreland Hill to get home.

'You are wasting your time, Miss,' he said, staring at Helen through the dancing snow flakes.

'Has the bus gone — I thought I had minutes in hand.'

'There won't be any bus.'

'Can't it get through?'

'Got as far as top of Foreland Hill — then skidded and overturned.'

'Oh — my . . .'

'Police and the doctor are up there now. What a mess . . . the bus is blocking the hill and the snowdrifts are coming down fast behind it.'

The man plodded past. Helen decided to get a taxi, but the local man refused to turn out. He was convinced that even if he got over as far as Highport he would not get back and he had no desire to be trapped in his car over the week-end.

'Take my advice and stay put in the village,' he advised Helen.

She grew more anxious as the minutes ticked past. There was of course a strong possibility that the

24

Channel Ferry would dock late because of the rough passage and difficulty in getting in to harbour, but she was alarmed at the prospect of Tommy spending Christmas in Highport while she remained in Haven Bay. Only a few miles separating the two places, but they might have been at opposite ends of the earth.

Helen knew of no other way in reaching the headland. Steve always reckoned it was quicker across the bay by boat than making the trip along the coastal road, but only a madman would venture out to sea on a night like this.

She could only hope that the blizzard would fade before morning, and the snow ploughs by working through the night would clear the road.

Perhaps then, she could catch the first bus out in the morning, although it meant depriving herself of the pleasure of meeting Tommy off the boat.

Reluctantly, she stepped across the road and went into the telephone box. If nothing else could be achieved that night, she must let Tommy know she could not travel.

Helen looked up the number of Chanline Shipping Company. They occupied four lines and Helen fed coins into the box. Each line was engaged and she spent more than ten minutes trying to get through to a receptionist to pass a message to Tommy. She could only assume that the company's switchboard was jammed.

She fumbled in her handbag for more coins, then the feeble light in the telephone box went out completely. She breathed a sigh of irritation, and in the pitch blackness she twirled the dial and got through to the operator. The line was terrible, but finally she managed to quote the number she wanted and asked for a reverse charge.

She had not met Tommy's family many times. During the couple's whirlwind courtship, Tommy was one for getting out and about. Theatre trips to London. Parties with the local young set and eating in Highport's plush restaurants was his idea of how to treat a girl.

But, Helen had telephoned him frequently during that time and she did know the number by heart.

Presently, the operator told her to go ahead and before she could say anything, the voice at the other end said:

'Helen!'

It sounded eerie attacking her like it did in the dark. She answered swiftly for fear of losing the line. The storm was playing havoc with the communications.

'Is that Mrs. Carr — Tommy's mother?'

The voice came back at her. Agitated, close to despair:

'Tommy's father is down at the harbour — now.'

'I don't understand . . .'

'My dear — we can only pray.'

Helen was stunned.

'What's happened?' she enquired weakly.

'She's gone down . . .'

'What!'

'The Channel Ferry — with Tommy on board. She's sunk!'

'My God,' murmured Helen.

'You haven't heard.'

The line went dead and Helen was left holding the receiver in her numbed hands.

It was impossible. The sleek white and gold ships ferried hundreds of thousands of passengers across the Channel during a normal year without mishap. Helen realised tonight was not ordinary with gale force winds and a blizzard hitting the Straits at the same time, but the ships' records spoke for themselves.

Even when the lifeboat was called, it had never occurred to Helen that it was the Channel Ferry that was in distress. She had suspected that a foreign vessel groping its way to the Port of London had run into difficulties, but never the reliable Ferry.

She came out of the telephone box as

28

if it was a dark tomb she had escaped from. She blamed herself for her indifference in attempting to meet the bus, when all the while, Tommy was out in that hateful stretch of water, fearing the worst.

She stepped knee-deep in snow, and where previously the whiteness had given light relief to the dark village, now it barely glimmered.

Helen realised that all the lights in the village were out. The snow thick and furious, ruthlessly smothered everything in sight.

She clawed her way back to the sea front. The corner shop was shut and a weather board rammed against the door. Helen lifted her eyes and saw the people lining the sea wall. Despite the blizzard, they had risked chills to come out of doors. Helen was convinced then, it was something serious.

She infiltrated the cluster of watchers, and stood close to a man's broad back. The villagers were muttering among themselves as they tried to discern any object on the heaving, savage sea.

A retired Naval officer had taken over at the lifeboat station, and was trying to get information from the coastguards at Highport. He clung on to the telephone and barked over the line. He had got so much and no more. The line went dead, and although he knew how to use the radio, he dare not for fear of butting in on a frequency that was open to any ship in distress.

He stamped out of the station, a short, chunky man with plum-red features.

'We can only wait and hope . . . the Ferry struck one of those wrecks that have cluttered up the shipping lane during this year. She's gone down.'

Someone in the crowd remarked that the lifeboat had been gone a long time, and the remark was left unanswered, although it gave many food for thought.

Helen wiped the wet snow out of her eyes. She shivered and was less hardy than these locals who had lived on this isolated, storm ravaged corner of the coast for the whole of their lives.

The villagers did not budge, and would wait until there was something they could do for the survivors, then it would be frantic action all the way.

They waited, concerned only for the poor devils out there on that merciless sea, and ignoring what was happening to the village.

The snow piled up on the coastal road. An overturned bus blocked one entrance to the village. Snowdrifts made the journey to Highport impossible.

The telephones were already dead. The coastguard at Highport was out of touch with the lifeboat station at Haven Bay.

The power had failed. The cottages were unlit, and candles and lamps were being salvaged from hidden corners. The sea front and the narrow High Street looked grotesque with the reflections of the slow flickering lights.

In that moment, there were many of the villagers who had someone at sea. Helen was fond of two men out there in the Channel, and she desperately prayed that both should return to her.

3

As the temperature dropped below freezing point, it was obvious that the villagers were doing no service to anyone lingering on the sea wall and staring blindly into the snow storm.

Helen ventured to treat the situation with common sense, and she spoke loudly enough for all to hear:

'We are sure to be needed before the night is over — but what use will we be if we are dog tired and chilled to the bone.'

The retired Naval officer who had taken charge of the lifeboat station agreed with Helen.

'Go home all of you. Get some food and rest, and I'll wait here. If I get any news, I'll fire a rocket.'

The crowd dispersed, and Helen found her way through the darkness to her lodgings.

Miss Pegler had refused to go to bed. Instead she sat it out by a small fire, grey-haired but active, and nothing of her long career in nursing forgotten. Helen observed that her elderly landlady had an old black bag packed and placed close to hand.

She was surprised by Helen's return.

'You left a note saying you were off to Highport . . .'

'I couldn't get through.'

Miss Pegler bounded out of the chair. She stoked the fire and bustled Helen to sit by it.

'You are frozen. Give me your coat and shoes. I'll fetch you a bowl of soup.'

Helen allowed herself to be half undressed. She warmed her chilled body by the glowing fire and fed well on the soup and toast that Miss Pegler brought her.

'Any news?' asked the landlady.

Helen shook her head.

'Commander Forbes is on duty at the station. If he gets any messages over the radio he'll call for help.'

Miss Pegler lit a second candle as the first began to melt.

'We are in a bit of a fix ourselves,' she declared.

'No power or communications,' reflected Helen.

'The lights are always the first to go,' said Miss Pegler.

Helen reached for her transistor set and switched it on.

'Maybe we won't feel so cut off listening to this.'

It was dismal listening. Tragedies up and down the country, but the villages that lined the Straits came in for special mention. The bus that had overturned at Foreland Hill came into the news bulletin, and then a special report from Highport concerning the Channel Ferry that had gone down. Survivors had been picked up from open boats when the ship had been abandoned, and were being landed at various points around the coast. The rescue operation was slow because the blizzard made it impossible for helicopters and air-rescue to be used. Everything depended upon the lifeboats who had raced to the rescue from a number of ports and harbours along the coast.

'Open boats — in this weather,' commented Helen, huskily.

'But, the lifeboats were out there quickly.'

Helen fidgeted with the transistor.

'It has been a long search. Why hasn't Steve got back?'

Miss Pegler gave Helen a look of concern.

'You must be suffering, my dear . . . the other boy, wasn't he crossing on the ferry, this evening?'

'I'm hoping that Steve might have some news,' confessed Helen, with a quiet nod.

'The Channel Ferry packs 'em in,' reflected Miss Pegler.

'I realise a lot of people will be praying to be picked up,' said Helen.

'You can bet your sweet life, Steve Day won't return to base empty handed . . .'

'Listen!' exclaimed Helen.

She had caught a strange wavelength while fiddling with her transistor, and a voice came through, loud and urgently:

'Lifeboat to Haven Bay . . .'

Helen jumped to her feet. She had picked up a message from the lifeboat. The message had obviously got through to Commander Forbes on duty in the station as well. Barely another minute elapsed before a rocket tore through the night sky and alerting the villagers with a loud 'crump'.

Helen slung a dry coat around her shoulders and shoved her feet into rubber boots, but she was no quicker in getting ready than her landlady. Miss Pegler donned her old nurse's gaberdine, picked up her bag and marched to the door.

'There'll be a job for everyone who wants one,' she decided.

Along the sea front, doors were flung open, lights were doused, and people shrugged off the spitefulness of the blizzard as they charged towards the lifeboat station.

Commander Forbes made the announcement that the lifeboat was on the way home with a boatload of survivors. He wanted men with shovels to clear the slipway, and women to prepare comforts for the survivors.

Helen suggested the the school was the best place to serve as a reception area. It was spacious and an up to date kitchen was attached to the school, even if the villagers did offer to take the survivors into their own cottages.

She was quickly joined by half a dozen women and together they trudged away from the sea front and along the hundred yards of Lower Road to the school.

Helen knocked up Judd the caretaker, the old seaman wasn't asleep, far from it, in fact he had kept up a ceaseless vigil ever since he had heard the first maroon explode in the air.

The caretaker was in the attic of his cottage next to the school, and he used the attic as an observation post complete with powerful telescope. He spent many hours during the day watching the shipping pass along the Straits, and although his eye was well trained, he had not spotted a thing on this blizzard torn night until a few seconds ago.

'Just a glimpse I got of her . . . but Steve's bringing her in,' he declared.

Helen confirmed that the lifeboat was heading for shore with survivors, and they were to be given shelter and food in the school.

'Will you unlock the school, Mr. Judd?'

The caretaker let them in and helped push the desks back against the walls and a spacious aisle was formed. The ladies boiled water while Judd foraged the premises for lamps and blankets. He knew where everything was kept and it wasn't the first time the school had been taken over by survivors from a wrecked vessel.

Helen had claimed a torch from her own desk, and when she was satisfied that all that could be done at the school was completed, she volunteered to return to the jetty on the sea front and lead the survivors to shelter.

On her way down she met the owner of the corner shop, who with the help of his two sons and his wife were hauling boxes of food along to the school.

'Reckon a few rations will come in handy,' he suggested to Helen.

'The gas is still on up at the school. The ladies will put the food to good use,' Helen assured him.

She fought her way down to the sea front and arrived at the slipway.

Steve had docked the lifeboat, and the hawsers were taut against the bollards on the jetty. There was a general air of relief and excitement that always accompanied the lifeboat's return, and Steve, his oilskins drenched seemed to stand out head and shoulders above everyone else. He had earned this image over the past three years, ever since he had been asked to take charge of the lifeboat.

He climbed ashore, and Helen was

quick to notice a change in him. He glowered fiercely and was short tempered with the willing Commander Forbes who had made a good job of running things while the lifeboat had been to sea.

'Aren't the police here?' he demanded.

The Commander glanced behind him at the remnants of the sizeable crowd, and reflected that he hadn't seen the local constable all night.

'He isn't here.'

Helen turned up her coat collar and trotted forward. The wind was fierce and the sea turbulent as she stood on the edge of the wall.

'Steve . . . thank goodness!'

She had an irresistible urge to touch him, to make certain he really had come back, but the scowling features put her off, and she felt shy in his presence.

'Who is supposed to be running things on shore?' he demanded.

'We have done our best.'

'My God — what a night!' groaned Steve.

'It is no picnic here,' Helen told him. 'We have no lights or power, and the telephones are dead. I fear we are cut off by the snowdrifts.'

'That isn't unusual,' he replied gruffly.

'Steve — what's the matter?'

He jerked his head at the boatload of survivors. The crew were having a job persuading them off the lifeboat and up the slipway.

'That boatload of trouble — that's the matter. Of all things to pick up . . . '

'But you saved them!'

'All but two or three are dead drunk. It nearly cost us our lives getting them aboard . . . they were playing the fool. Think of it — playing the fool while we were transferring them from the cutter to the lifeboat.'

'Who are they?'

'I haven't had time to find out. But, I would have felt happier if the police had been here.'

Helen said slowly:

'I believe the constable is cut off

outside the village. He and Dr. Marsh went to an accident, and I can't see any way they could have got back.'

In the pitch blackness the survivors trooped ashore. They had been rescued in what they stood up in. There had not been time to desert the sinking ferry with their luggage, and some were not wearing top coats. So drunk were the majority of them, that they had been insensible to the danger they were in when the ferry struck the unchartered wreck. Afterwards, they became panic stricken and wild, some of them resisting the helping hands from the lifeboat crew when the rescue operation got under way.

Despite the freezing weather, not all were sober yet. There was much cursing, swaying and tripping over mounds in the ice capped snow, as the survivors tried to feel dry land beneath their feet.

Steve's patience was sorely tried.

'Let's get 'em under shelter.'

'I have made room along the school,' said Helen.

'Food is being prepared . . . '

'The lifeboat crew will be glad of a hot meal. But, I reckon the survivors will just want to sleep it off,' replied Steve.

'Can the drunks make it to the school?' queried Helen.

'They will damn well have to . . . nothing on four wheels will skate across this snowbound surface.'

Helen and Steve went ahead of the untidy procession. The survivors groped for support and followed blindly.

Helen ventured to say:

'About Tommy . . . what are the chances?'

'Everyone on board the ferry, tonight, stands a good chance of getting rescued. The traffic out there was thick, and the ferry, she went down gracefully giving the lifeboats chance to reach her.'

'Thank you,' murmured Helen.

'It is the truth,' said Steve. 'I am not just being kind.'

They reached the school, bravely lit with oil lamps and candles. Blankets were laid out on the floor, and the smell of food escaped from the kitchen.

The survivors collapsed groaning to the floor, clawing for the comfort of the blankets.

Steve regarded them with displeasure, still smarting from the trouble they had given him.

'Made pigs of themselves on duty free liquor,' he commented. 'Seen so many tourists parties like it. They make a bee line for the ship's bars the instant they get aboard.'

'Some of them look really ill,' observed Helen.

'Yeah . . . we shall have to fetch Jimmy Marsh. He won't thank us for allowing this mob to catch pneumonia, even if they aren't helping themselves.'

'Young Dr. Marsh is out of the village. Miss Pegler is about somewhere,' said Helen.

'They need a doctor,' decided Steve.

Helen looked at him squarely.

'I'll go and fetch old Dr. Marsh.'

Steve held Helen by her shoulders.

'I am going to depend on you a lot, Helen. We work well together, and I am not happy with this situation.'

'I am here to help,' confirmed Helen. 'I'll not brood over Tommy all the while I am busy.'

'I assure you, Helen — if anyone was lost from the ferry, then it was damn clumsy.'

'How long will I be kept waiting for news, though?'

'I tell you what I'm going to do,' said Steve. 'As soon as the doctor has examined the survivors, we'll get their names and addresses. The shipping company at Highport will want details to give to next of kin.'

'But we have no telephones . . . '

'I'll open up a wavelength on the radio to the coastguard station. They will pass on the information.'

'Perhaps we can get some information about Tommy from them,' suggested Helen.

'Possibly,' agreed Steve.

As it turned out, there was no need for Dr. Marsh, Snr, to be called. He reported to the school, heavily muffled, after getting up from bed where he was fighting off a chill. Miss Pegler came in with him.

The doctor took one glance at the stupified survivors, and wrinkled his nose at the air tainted with alcohol fumes.

'Let's get them into dry clothing,' he said.

Miss Pegler sniffed haughtily.

'It would serve them right if we left them to fend for themselves,' she declared.

4

There were plenty of volunteers to see that the survivors were made comfortable, and the large coal fire in the classroom was stoked continuously.

Steve realised it was vital to have them identified, and while Helen did her best to extract information from the survivors, all she got for her pains were foolish smiles, stupid jokes or plain abuse.

Steve would stand for no nonsense, and he swooped on them, demanding passports. He gave them no chance to resist and swiftly read the passport entries. Helen found an exercise book and between them they compiled a list.

'Let's get down to the lifeboat station and use the radio,' said Steve.

Helen closed the exercise book, and saw that Miss Pegler and a trio of helpers were preparing for a session of night duty.

A couple of the survivors were actually ill and although they slept, Dr. Marsh wanted to be called when they awoke. Under the circumstances, Miss Pegler was not going to be allowed to stay alone.

'We can do no more until morning,' assumed Helen.

She was gently ushered out of doors. The blizzard had died down, but the snow was being lifted off the headland in gusts and smothering the road all the way to Haven Bay. The sky was sullen with storm and snow.

They returned to the sea front. The lifeboat was safely housed after being hauled up the slipway by the power winches. Steve invited Helen through to his living quarters, and saw that she was comfortable in a chair by the fire before he took the exercise book from her and made to open up the radio link.

Although Steve's family lived four doors away from Miss Pegler's cottage, Steve set up quarters for himself during the winter months. His single bed, large cabin trunk, the square table with the radio on it, and a collection of books looked a jumble to Helen, as Steve tried to combine his living and working quarters.

'Not much room,' he apologised, 'but I don't like being far away when the telephone rings.'

Helen loosened her coat and watched Steve tune in the radio. He got through to the coastguard at Highport, and Helen considered it to be a frail link, just two voices connecting the tiny village in the bay with the dominant headland.

Steve passed on the information about his survivors, and then the coastguard made conversation about the massive rescue operation that a score of lifeboats along the coast had launched.

The number of survivors landed was encouraging news, and when Steve spoke in a low voice, mentioning the name of Tommy Carr, Helen sat up with a jerk.

While a reply was awaited, Steve gave details concerning the plight of the village. Cut off by snowdrifts in both directions, Haven Bay was without lights and telephones. The police constable and young Dr. Marsh were stranded outside the village, while the twenty-two survivors, although well cared for, were too sorry for themselves to be of any use.

'How you off for food?' asked the coastguard.

'Might be a problem if we are snowbound for several days,' Steve admitted.

The corner shop stocked modestly, having given way a long time ago to Highport's attractive shopping centre.

'What about fuel?'

Steve reported that created no worries. The villagers held their winter stocks of coal for their open fires.

'I reckon you have got yourself an emergency, Steve,' commented the coastguard. 'I'll hurry along the snow ploughs.'

'It isn't exclusively my emergency,' protested Steve. 'I'm only the lifeboat-man who can handle the radio.'

The coastguard did not agree.

'Take charge, Steve. Otherwise it'll be chaos, especially with strangers in the village.'

Steve grunted, and went on listening while the coastguard concluded his message.

Helen waited tensely for news about Tommy. Steve closed down the radio then turned to Helen.

'Nothing so far about Tommy. But, it is early days.'

'I see.'

'If anything comes through, I'll let you know, instantly . . . '

The following morning there was much to do in the village, although with the temperature below freezing and a bitter wind blowing straight in from the sea, the villagers would have loved to have stayed indoors and nursed their open fires.

Helen had managed a few hours

sleep and was awoken when Miss Pegler came home, after her all night stint at the school looking after the survivors.

The old nurse was fast asleep when Helen ventured out of doors. The snow was falling lightly, but by the appearance of the sullen sky over the Channel, heavier snow was on the way. It was an unpleasant prospect with the wind so harsh in the Straits.

Helen trudged up to the school, and she observed that the cluster of shops in the High Street, the small village post office included, had not opened their doors for the day's business, although it was past nine-thirty a.m.

She had passed the lifeboat station, and it appeared deserted. Helen guessed that Steve was on his rounds of the village seeing what ought to be done. He had made it plain to Helen, last night, that the village without light or means of communication, except by the fragile link of the radio, must be considered to be in a state of emergency.

He had assumed control of the village, and his first job was to warn the shopkeepers not to sell goods to the residents. If the village remained cut off for the next few days, there would be a need for rationing.

Helen saw the first example of Steve's determination to get something done about the snowdrifts. A party of husky young men from the sea front armed with picks and shovels were heading in the direction of Foreland Hill to attempt to force a way through.

One of them called out to her:

'Steve's been asking after you!'

'Where is he?'

'Up at the school, I reckon.'

Helen's heart pounded. Perhaps, he had received a signal from the headland coastguard station that Tommy had now been named among the survivors.

Her step increased, even if it was a hard slog through the snow, but she felt that her advance to the school had more purpose, now.

It was a sombre scene in the

classroom. The survivors were huddled round the fire, all of them very seedy-looking, and trying to force down the breakfast that the women volunteers had served from the kitchen.

Steve was in earnest conversation with Dr. Marsh, who looked flushed with the effect of the chill that he had been unable to shake off.

He was not slow in observing Helen's sprightly entrance, however, and he smiled in a way that gave hope to her.

Dr. Marsh took himself away to his bed to steal a few hours sleep. He intended holding a surgery at noon, and to visit the survivors afterwards. Two of them were suffering from exposure and giving the doctor cause for anxiety. He would have desired them to be in hospital beds, instead of the discomfort of the classroom floor.

Helen approached Steve, without delay.

'Any news of Tommy?'

He shook his head. That wasn't what he wanted to see her about.

'I opened up the radio at six a.m. The list of survivors hadn't been completed. Relatives have been telephoning High-port all night for information apparently.'

'That's no use here. We haven't a telephone that is alive,' protested Helen.

'Be patient,' urged Steve.

Helen sighed and nodded.

'You wanted to see me?'

'Yes — I would have called at your cottage, but I didn't want to risk disturbing Miss Pegler. She had a tough night.'

'You have a job for me?'

'We have got to find billets for these survivors. It isn't comfortable enough at the school. We may have to put up with them for the rest of the week, at least.'

Helen understood what was needed. She would have to make door to door visits, asking the villagers if they had any spare room.

'I'll make a start, right away,' she promised.

'About Tommy,' mentioned Steve. 'I'll get in touch with the coastguard again as soon as I have a minute to spare.'

He glanced in the direction of the sullen survivors, decided they would be alright for a while, and then accompanied Helen out of doors.

'I'm off down to the shops to see what stocks they have on hand,' explained Steve.

He was aware that Helen was quiet, and he realised she was feeling depressed about Tommy. He hoped he would have some good news to tell her, later on, but meanwhile he trusted that she would be too busy in her capacity as billeting officer to waste time brooding.

Helen made a tour of the sea front cottages, and was surprised at the resistance she met. The villagers had always opened their hearts and their front doors to survivors, but they were frankly disgusted with the boatload that had been brought ashore, last night.

'Hooligans and drunkards. Would you invite them into your home?' Helen was asked on a number of occasions.

Helen admitted that the party of tourists had been foolish but once they sobered up, nobody would have any bother. But, there was no comfort at the school, and the men would be bored stiff staying there, while two were genuinely sick.

She used all her charm and finally managed to obtain rooms for all but one.

'Providing they behave themselves, I'll take a couple,' agreed her last call.

Helen wondered if Miss Pegler would provide a room for the odd man out. She carried on along to the end of the short sea front, and went in to the cottage where she lodged.

Miss Pegler was up, but looking very weary. She had promised to go and help Dr. Marsh with his surgery at noon, as the regular receptionist lived up at Foreland Hill and wasn't able to get into the village.

Helen knew that the old nurse was no more keen on the type of survivor that had been landed, than any of the other villagers, but she cast her resentment aside, and told Helen she would make room for one.

'See if you can fix it so that one of the sick men comes here. One of them is young . . . I did feel sorry for him.'

Helen ticked off the final name on her list, then retraced her steps.

The snow was falling fast, and she hurried back to the school. Steve had given word that the survivors were going to be found accommodation in the village, and the volunteer helpers, together with Judd the caretaker were clearing up the disorderly classroom.

Helen tried to make friends with the survivors, encouraging them with the news that they were leaving the bare surroundings for the cosiness of a home with a villager.

She found it difficult to cheer up men who were suffering from hangovers, and she quickly led them away from the school to the various cottages, where they were taken in.

The two survivors suffering from severe exposure had to be left behind until arrangements could be made to carry them to their billets.

Helen called in upon Steve. He was working the radio, and she stopped in the doorway until he had finished receiving the message.

He closed down and then sat still, staring at the radio set. It was several seconds before he realised that Helen was there.

Helen warded off the suspense by declaring that billets for all the survivors had been found, but she wanted help to get the sick couple carried out of the school.

'They are too feverish to walk . . . '

'Wait, Helen!' interrupted Steve.

'This is important,' argued Helen.

She was whistling in the dark and Steve knew it.

'Come in and sit down.'

'I haven't time . . . '

'Helen,' said Steve, crisply. 'Please sit down.'

She walked meekly into his living quarters, stared across at him, and waited in fear.

'It is bad news, isn't it?'

Steve nodded.

'The list of survivors is complete — Tommy is not among them.'

Helen sat in silence. She could not weep, but felt sick with a shivering sensation that attacked her like a savage wind. Her nerves were ragged, and she could not suffer Steve, watching her with a pitying expression on his rugged features.

Helen knew she offended him when she cried out:

'The damn spiteful sea. How I hate it!'

Steve let her go on giving furious vent to her feelings. He was certain it helped relieve her tension, but she refused to weep in front of him.

'I have asked them over at Highport to check the lists,' he said.

'People don't make mistakes on anything as vital as this,' said Helen.

'It is too early to give up hope,' insisted Steve.

'If only we were not confined to the four sides of this tiny village. I can't get out ... to see for myself. To visit Tommy's family. A convict in Dartmoor is better off than we are,' she protested.

Steve was not callous enough to try and step into a dead man's shoes, but he was convinced that Helen wanted someone's help. If she could only ignore his love and respect for the sea, and the part he played along this fiery quarter of the coast. But, he knew she would not accept him in her present mood.

He repeated his advice that it was too early to give up hope, but Helen drew his attention to a fresh blizzard that was attacking the village.

'What hope — in this weather.'

5

Helen quit the lifeboat station in a mood that shared grief with resentment, and she felt the need to be left on her own.

Steve thought she had gone mad when she ventured no farther than the sea wall. She stared out at the hostile sea, apparently oblivious to the fearful weather that struck through her clothes and stung her exposed face.

He pulled open the door to pursue her and make her listen to common sense. The blizzard screamed in on him, and he framed himself in the doorway and yelled at Helen:

'What are you trying to prove?'

Helen ignored him. She was numbed, not from the savage onslaught of the vile weather, but the sadness of Tommy's loss. There was frustration too, being trapped in this little village and not knowing the truth of what happened outside.

Steve dashed out and grabbed her arm.

'Come on out of it!'

'Leave me alone!' she retorted passionately.

'I want to help you, Helen.'

'You can do nothing for me.'

They yelled in each other's faces. Steve was taken by surprise at her last comment.

'We have been friends for a long time.'

'You never understood what Tommy and I shared,' said Helen.

'Give me a chance to understand?' pleaded Steve.

'What is it you want, Steve — love on the rebound. I don't think you could catch me at the first bounce.'

'Neither of us want that.'

Helen wriggled out of his grasp.

'I have no affection to show anyone at this moment.'

'I'm not concerned with that . . . but

I won't allow you to stand out here and catch pneumonia.'

He grabbed her again and forced her under shelter.

'You are wet through,' added Steve.

'Stop acting like a wet nurse.'

Steve was unable to fathom out this young woman who was famous in the village for her sweet nature, but then, he had met tragedy on several occasions and learned to live with it. For Helen, it came like a savage blow from the unknown.

The flickering of a red lamp on the radio set forced him to break off the conflict, and he slumped in front of the set to take a message from the coastguard over at the headland.

Helen stood there breathing heavily. The signal from Highport calmed her, and she waited anxiously. Maybe, after all there was hope.

She was condemned to disappointment. Steve was being informed that the snow ploughs had given up the task of clearing the roads that day with the arrival of a fresh blizzard.

Foreland Hill was posing problems because the overturned bus had not yet been towed away, and the snow plough could not get past.

Weather conditions were too bad for flying, and Steve could not expect help from helicopters.

He argued that he had two sick men who ought to be in hospital, but there was nothing anybody could do, and the weather forecast was bleak.

As Steve was talking, his own working party who had attempted to dig a way out of the village, trooped home. They had chipped at the solid ice for several hours, but when a minor avalanche descended upon them, they retreated.

Steve closed down the set, and turned to Helen.

'I shall have to make arrangements for the two sick men to be moved into more comfortable quarters.'

'I am going to look after one of them,' declared Helen.

'That might be a good thing,' remarked Steve.

The survivor billeted upon Miss Pegler was a pleasant faced young man, whose lack of fight against his condition was worrying.

His name was Jim West, and his passport showed an address in East London, while his photograph depicted a cheerfully smiling character who wore a cheeky expression in his eyes.

'That's how we have to get you to look like again,' murmured Helen, as she looked down at the patient in the small back room of Miss Pegler's cottage.

Miss Pegler was too busy helping Dr. Marsh to attend exclusively to Jim, so she challenged Helen to take on the responsibility.

It was what Helen needed at such a time, and as the patient required rest and feeding with liquid foods with perhaps the attention of a pretty nurse to boost his morale, she was capable of taking on the task.

Miss Pegler showed Helen how to

take Jim's temperature, and left instructions for his proper nursing.

She showed Jim her undivided attention. When the fever rose in his body, she sat by the bedside, drying the perspiration from his face.

She fed him on beef tea by spoon, and looked into his vacant expression for a sign of hope. There was none, and the young man was content to collapse into the pillows after his meal.

As darkness fell, Jim started to babble in his delirium. Helen took his temperature and peered at the minute figures by the light of an oil lamp. His temperature was rising. Helen found yet another blanket, and stoked up the open fire in the bedroom.

The hot fever attacked him, and left alone, Helen had to hold him down. Suddenly, it became the most important thing in her life, that she should not fail her patient.

Jim fought with her and despite his sickness he was strong. Helen needed help, but realised none would be forthcoming. Miss Pegler had gone on a call with Dr. Marsh, and of course, the telephone in the hall was useless.

She found she could not match him for physical strength, so she did her utmost to humour and soothe him.

Helen stroked his hot brow, and whispered his name. Then after one angry shout, his words became less muddled. He sank back exhausted, stared at the ceiling and spoke dreamily but openly.

Helen continued to humour him, and once, when he aimed a mistrustful look at her, she threw caution to the winds and kissed him lightly.

He smiled and gained confidence in the young woman by his bedside. Jim held out his hand. Helen took it. Then, without another word he fell asleep.

Helen stayed for another hour, then when she was satisfied the fever had passed, she crept back to her own room, and did not stir until Miss Pegler opened the front door, and climbed the stairs.

In the morning, Jim sat up in bed and gave Helen a warm smile.

'I am ravenous,' he announced.

'That is good news. I'll go and cook your breakfast.'

'What is your name?'

'Helen Foster.'

'You are a splendid nurse,' Jim told her.

'I am not really a nurse.'

Jim was surprised at her admission.

'I looked into your face, last night — and saw an angel,' he said.

'Nonsense,' retorted Helen.

'It is true . . . but if you are not a nurse, then what do you do?'

'I teach twenty-five infants here at the village school.'

'That explains it. You do care about people!'

'Why yes — that's true.'

'And you kissed me?'

'Just to reassure you that you were in good hands,' answered Helen.

Jim nodded solemnly.

'It worked then. It was marvellous to feel wanted again.'

Helen could hear the kettle singing off its head downstairs and she darted into the kitchen, spent twenty minutes preparing Jim his breakfast on a tray, then took it up to his room.

'Tuck into this,' she invited him.

Jim waited until she placed the tray across him in the bed, then he urged that she should come back when he had finished the meal.

'I want to talk,' he said.

Helen let it slip that he had done enough talking last night to satisfy any public speaker for a month.

'You ought to rest,' she concluded.

But, when she returned to the room a little while afterwards to collect his tray, Jim said:

'I reckon you heard it all?'

Helen kept her face averted.

'It made sense — in between the babbling,' she admitted.

'I meant what I said, Helen. It was marvellous to feel wanted.'

'Don't let one friendly kiss go to your head, Jim.'

'Didn't you enjoy it?'

The cheeky expression that was so noticeable in his passport photograph suddenly dominated his features.

'I haven't thought about it since.'

'We could be friends,' suggested Jim.

Helen gave him a tender glance.

'Haven't you got problems enough?'

'I lost Peggy to another man — and my job, all within a week,' confessed Jim. 'I'm willing to write off my past experiences if I can see something of a future in front of me.'

'Don't ask me to help pick up your pieces, Jim.'

'Do I sound pitiful? I wasn't making a go at it as a high pressure salesman, while Peggy was going ahead with her career as a secretary. We had this flat, and were saving like mad to buy a house. We planned to have children within five years.'

'Sounds cut and dried,' commented Helen.

'Peggy found the invitations from her boss too tempting. An offer to accompany him on a business conference in

Brussels before Christmas was just too much. She suggested I got rid of the flat, and she would pursue her own life. She gave our marriage a minute's notice, and I got the same treatment from my firm.'

'It happens too often,' said Helen. 'How did you end up on the cross-Channel ferry in a blizzard?'

'Some of the lads in the Rugby Club planned this trip to the Paris night spots, and because I felt so low, I joined them.'

'Did it do any good — drowning your sorrows?'

'It was stupid. I'm ashamed I got drunk — and I could have seen better night spots in Soho.'

'You landed in a mess,' observed Helen.

'If I could have met someone like you, last week . . . '

'Jim — you won't be the first man who thinks he has fallen for his nurse.'

'I have this feeling, Helen. You are not catching me on the rebound, if that is what you think.'

Helen moved towards the door.

'Perhaps not — but I fear, you could be catching me — first bounce.'

Jim sat up in bed. He winced where the bruises reminded him of his heavy fall into the open boat when he had jumped from the ferry, and he caught his breath before speaking.

'You have problems, too?'

Helen shrugged.

'I am alright, Jim.'

He was insistent.

'If you don't tell me — I'll find out. This seems to be a pretty small village — the sort of place where nobody can keep a secret.'

Helen turned back. She wanted no sympathy from Jim, and it was never her intention to join him as a fellow loser. There was something in common however, with this young survivor and Tommy Carr. They had both been on the ferry when it had started to flounder.

'What was it like on that boat in that

dreadful storm, Jim?'

Jim curled his lip.

'I don't remember much . . . would probably have taught me a lesson if I had been aware of what was going on.'

'Was there panic?'

'Yes — plenty of that. The boat was pretty full.'

'But, there were enough lifeboats to go round.'

'I can't say . . . but why all these questions?'

Helen was tongue-tied for a moment, then becoming supremely optimistic, she hurried into her room, collected her bedside photograph of Tommy and took it into Jim's room to show him.

'I suppose there is no chance of you remembering seeing this man on the boat?'

Jim wanted desperately to help Helen, but all the faces around him at the bar on the boat were his chums in the Rugby Club, and the patient bartenders who poured them drinks.

'I'm sorry, Helen,' he said, gravely

handing her the photograph. 'I just wouldn't know . . . '

Helen held the photograph against her heart.

'It was an awful long shot,' she admitted.

Jim realised what Helen's problem amounted to, and he felt as if he wanted to tear the world apart to find Tommy for her.

'You have had no news of him?'

Helen shook her head.

'It is so frustrating — being cooped up in this village.'

Jim regarded her earnestly.

'You probably saved my life, last night. Nursing me, unselfishly, yet all the time, you suffered . . . '

'I find it less cruel if I am too busy to brood about it,' said Helen.

'I reckon we do need each other,' declared Jim.

Helen took the photograph back to her room, then leaving Jim to rest, she went downstairs.

She was pottering in the kitchen

when Steve called on her to see if she was managing to remain tight-lipped about her personal tragedy. He hadn't noticed her in the village since she had gone home yesterday at noon, and wondered if she could do with his company.

Steve was certain there were faint traces of tears in her eyes, but Helen spoke without grief.

'I have been busy nursing Jim West. He's on the way to recovery, and I guess it has given me enough satisfaction not to worry about anything else.'

Steve nodded, and after expressing his pleasure that Helen was fully occupied, he departed.

6

Miss Pegler returned to the cottage after Dr. Marsh's surgery finished at ten-thirty a.m. She visited Jim before she took a well earned rest, and congratulated Helen on doing such a fine job overnight.

Helen could see that the old nurse was suffering from fatigue, and she asked if there was anything she could do.

'I understand Steve Day has arranged for the shops to open. Goods will be restricted to each customer to prevent hoarding, so perhaps you would like to do the shopping,' Miss Pegler, suggested.

Helen collected a shopping bag, put on her rubber boots and trudged through the snow to the corner shop at the end of the sea front.

There was a lull in the snowfall, but

the sky looked bleak. The high tide smacked against the sea wall, and the Channel was empty of shipping.

In the absence of the local constable, Steve had called up his lifeboat crew to stand by to maintain law and order, and they were keeping an eye on the queue at the corner shop, while in the High Street, the local tobacconist was serving one packet of cigarettes each to his customers.

The survivors, after being segregated when they were billeted to the cluster of sea front cottages, now joined up again in a mob.

They were restless and discontented. The main reason being, they were in every case, down to their last few pence. By pooling their frugal cash, they were however able to purchase a few packets of cigarettes, and then had a general share out.

There was some ugly squabbling while the share out was being conducted, and Steve was about to intervene when the differences among the men were settled.

He was not certain the next meeting of the men would pass off so quietly, and the latest information he had received from Highport, warned that the blizzard would return yet again before nightfall, and the village would remain cut off for three more days.

The prospect made Steve uneasy. The villagers, he felt could take it, but the survivors, homesick, fed-up and broke, not received too readily by the residents could be on the verge of a rebellion.

Steve spotted Helen in the queue at the corner shop and he strode over to join her.

'Can we talk, Helen?'

'Is it personal?'

'Not this time.'

'Alright, then.'

'The survivors . . . '

'A surly lot, aren't they,' commented Helen, looking at them as they trudged morosely along the sea front.

'They must feel like prisoners.'

'Don't we all,' said Helen.

'They haven't a bean between them.'

'If we are cut off for many more days, there will be nothing left for anyone to buy. Money will be quite useless,' remarked Helen.

'The shopkeepers have taken stock. If we are careful there are enough provisions to last for a week.'

'The weather doesn't look like lifting,' observed Helen.

Steve grunted.

'I have been calling for a helicopter to take off the sick man — he hasn't made the recovery that your patient has — but everything has been grounded up to now.'

'Did you only want to discuss the general situation, Steve?'

Steve was aware of her impatience. She had changed since receiving the tragic news about Tommy Carr, and if she wouldn't allow him to show her the kindness he wanted to, Steve felt that his hands were tied.

Never before had he experienced

uneasiness in her presence, but he suffered from it now.

'No — I feel sorry for these chaps, flat broke and away from home.'

'What do you suggest?'

'The Seamen's Fund. I am sure there is enough in the kitty to provide the survivors with a few comforts.'

The Fund had been set up five years ago by the residents of Haven Bay, and during the past year, Steve and Helen had put in a lot of hard work boosting it by organising dances and other fund raising enterprises.

Helen, who was the current treasurer, said reflectively:

'There was almost two hundred pounds in deposit at the Post Office at the last Committee meeting.'

'We could afford a few quid and give the survivors a pay out,' urged Steve.

'Commander Forbes is the Chairman of the Fund . . .'

'Right — I'll see him.'

Steve looked closely at Helen. There seemed nothing more to say, except that he loved her, and if she would only let him behave towards her, even as her best friend, it would be reassuring.

But, Steve was convinced that Helen was going in the wrong direction. She had almost insisted that her concern lay with young Jim West, now resting in the small back room of the cottage where Helen lived, and that she was prepared to shut herself within the four walls, and show indifference to the problems that presented themselves to Haven Bay.

Helen had been of immense help to Steve in the past, and her loyalty to the lifeboat crew was almost as great as the only full-time member.

She returned Steve's intent look and asked:

'Anything else?'

'I have heard that the survivors are not getting on too well with their hosts.'

'Does it surprise you, Steve?'

'This village has a reputation of being kind to survivors.'

'Can you blame them for not

opening out their arms to a boatload of drunkards and hooligans?'

'They aren't all like that!'

'No,' admitted Helen. 'Jim West is very likeable.'

'But, he was drunk!'

'Jim had a reason . . . '

'Alright, Helen. Let's face facts. If we are all going to be cooped up in the village together, then we ought to try and get along. What about arranging a dance to break the ice?'

Helen told him, rather wearily:

'Steve, you know what's wanted in the village. Go ahead and do it.'

'You don't want to help?'

'I am hardly in the right frame of mind for dancing — or helping to run one.'

'This is an odd situation, Helen.'

'I know you have declared a state of emergency, Steve — but surely a woman is still allowed to have feelings.'

Steve nodded.

'Sure, I'm sorry. I'll do it on my own.'

He moved away, and Helen took her turn at the counter. Rationing wasn't strict, but the shopkeeper kept his eyes open in case there was any panic buying. The only shortage appeared to be in the supply of torches, batteries and candles, while oil for lamps was dwindling.

She returned along the sea front, and it was snowing again. The visibility in the Channel was down to nothing.

Jim's recovery sped along the true course of a normally healthy man, and now the fever was out of his body, he was ambitious enough to get on his feet.

'I'd like to get out and breathe the fresh air,' he told Helen, as she took him his lunch.

'Not in this weather, you don't.'

'I feel terrific . . . nothing on my mind.'

'You can come downstairs after lunch,' invited Helen.

'Are you staying indoors?'

'Of course — no sense in going out in the snow.'

'What shall we do?'

Helen shrugged.

'Play cards, listen to my transistor . . .'

'We can talk.'

'If you like,' agreed Helen.

Later in the afternoon, when the darkness was already falling, Helen and Jim sat on opposite sides of the fireplace and simply talked.

They were disturbed once, when one of the lifeboatmen turned up with an envelope addressed to Jim. It was obvious that Steve had arranged the pay out to the survivors, and each man was given two pounds. There was also a note in the envelope, advertising the dance to be held the following evening at the village school.

Jim held the envelope aloft and beamed at Helen.

'Pay day and an invitation to a dance. What more can a man wish for?'

Helen approved of his enthusiasm. At least, he was getting the sad experience of the past week out of his mind.

'This isn't a bad village to be stranded in, I suppose,' she remarked.

Jim came and sat beside her, instead of taking up his seat opposite.

'Can I take you to the dance, Helen?'

'Jim — you were hot with fever, last night. Now, you talk about dancing!'

'It is tomorrow evening. I shall be perfectly fit by then.'

'That is what you think. Dr. Marsh will be calling tomorrow morning. He will decide what is best for you.'

Jim leaned forward, and in the darkness his forehead brushed Helen's hair.

'If I am passed fit — will you come?'

'I can't . . . '

'Helen — if it's because of Tommy . . . '

'I must show respect, Jim.'

'You don't know for certain what has happened to him.'

'His name wasn't included in the list of survivors,' pointed out Helen.

'But, that is all you have to go by.'

'How else can I be sure? Ferry boats don't check names of passengers going aboard. They just accept a ticket and that's an end to it,' Helen reminded him, then she added reflectively: 'I was going to meet Tommy off of the boat. The boat was sunk and there has been no evidence that Tommy was rescued.'

'You have no evidence that he is lost, either,' Jim told her.

'I know that . . . '

Jim remembered the boarding procedure on the cross-Channel boat. It was true, for the short trip lists of passengers were not kept, but every ticket issued had a number, and it was possible for the ship's captain to know exactly how many passengers his boat was carrying.

'Has there been any news how many passengers are missing?' he challenged Helen.

'I don't see that is important. Tommy promised me he would be on the ferry.'

She could see that Jim was trying to give her morale a boost by his reasoning, and he was insistent that without firm news of Tommy's fate, then she had no cause to give up hope.

'If I were you, Helen — I would ask Steve Day to contact Highport, and tackle the problem from another angle.'

Helen bit her lip, and she had to admit that Jim's optimism filled her with fresh hope.

'You mean, find out how many passengers were not accounted for?'

'Exactly. The shipping company won't be able to supply names of those missing, but by now they would have had enquiries from relatives, and they will obviously put two and two together.'

Helen got to her feet.

'Tommy's parents live in Highport. They surely would have made enquiries . . . oh! If only I could have got across to the headland.'

She reached for her coat, and stepped into her rubber boots. Jim watched her run out of the cottage, and listened to her muffled footsteps ploughing through the deep snow.

Helen arrived breathlessly at the

lifeboat station. Steve was on duty. A replacement cross-Channel ferry was making for Highport, and having a rough passage. He could barely see the boat's lights as he squinted through his binoculars at the snow billowing across the sea.

Steve moved away from the window, and was curious to see the excitement in Helen's eyes.

'Steve,' she cried. 'Do you know how many passengers were posted as missing from the shipwreck.'

'The final figures are not out yet. The shipping company is still working on them.'

'Isn't it possible . . . ?'

'What are you trying to say, Helen?'

'Wouldn't it be a blessing — if Tommy wasn't aboard when the ferry sank?'

'Yes,' nodded Steve. 'A blessing!'

'When will you be contacting Highport again?'

'Shortly.'

'Do it now, please?'

'I can't, Helen. I must keep the wavelength clear until the ferry docks.'

'How much longer?'

Steve pulled a face.

'In these conditions — another hour before she enters harbour.'

'Can I wait?'

'Of course!'

She withdrew to Steve's living quarters, leaving him watching the unhappy progress of the ferry.

When the hour was up, the ferry still had not docked, and another twenty minutes went past before Steve lowered the binoculars.

'She's home and dry,' he announced.

Helen grew tense as Steve got through to Highport. He spent longer than usual in conversation with the headland coastguard, and Helen heard him ask the coastguard to check again on some detail.

Finally he came away from the radio set, and faced Helen with a mysterious expression on his face.

'The lifeboat crews all along the coast

have reason to be proud of their work, the other night,' he declared. 'The shipping company have announced, that not one passenger was lost.'

Helen's heart leapt with joy.

'If all are accounted for — then what about Tommy?'

'He could have missed the boat,' concluded Steve.

7

Helen kicked off her rubber boots and warmed her feet by Steve's fire. She looked relaxed, and was willing to look on the bright side of the situation, once more.

'It is marvellous to see you smile again,' commented Steve, as he handed Helen a mug of coffee.

'I feel such a fool,' admitted Helen.

'Why?'

'I took it for granted that because Tommy's name did not appear on the list of survivors, then he was forced to be lost at sea.'

'It was natural,' said Steve.

'But, he's not missing,' exclaimed Helen. 'Isn't it wonderful!'

'I'm pleased for you, Helen. I didn't like the way you were changing.'

'Tommy might be on that ferry that has just docked,' observed Helen.

'More than likely, if he missed the ferry that went down.'

'What a miracle . . . '

She lowered her voice and became subdued again.

'There can't be any mistakes, can there, Steve?'

'The shipping company are very meticulous in cases like this.'

'It is just that I don't think I could bear a second shock.'

Steve laid the plain facts before her.

'Tommy's name didn't appear among the survivors — but nobody was lost. Put two and two together, and that adds up to every passenger aboard the ferry was saved.'

Helen sighed deeply.

'Isn't it frustrating. Tommy could be home by now — and worrying what's happened to me. And, I am here — worrying about him.'

'Just six miles between you,' agreed Steve.

'How much longer are we likely to be stranded!' protested Helen.

'Clearing the road is at a standstill,' reported Steve, 'and we can't expect any help from the helicopter, while the visibility is so awful.'

'Things could get worse,' said Helen.

'I have been thinking,' murmured Steve.

'Yes?'

'Watching the cross-Channel ferry just now make that safe arrival. I think if matters don't improve here shortly — then I'll risk taking the lifeboat across the bay to Highport.'

Helen regarded the rugged young man, and a gentle expression invaded her features.

'That would be a risk, Steve.'

'It is a risk every time I take the boat out. If I could reach Highport, then I could bring back food and essential provisions — perhaps some engineers to fix up some lighting.'

Helen saw how determined Steve was about the proposed mission, and since she no longer held a gloomy view concerning Tommy's absence, she pleaded with him to take her with him to the headland.

Steve shook his head.

'It wouldn't be a trip for a girl, Helen.'

'But, how much longer must I put up with this suspense?'

'I'll tell you what. I will try and get some information from Highport whether or not Tommy has turned up. His business and his home are in the town, and if he did catch the ferry that has just berthed, then we ought to put your mind at rest.'

'This waiting for something to happen,' grumbled Helen. 'It is tearing my nerves to pieces.'

'Try not to think about it,' suggested Steve.

She emptied her mug of coffee, then decided she ought to get back home to see to her patient.

'How is he?' asked Steve.

'Pretty fit. He wants to go dancing, tomorrow evening.'

'Rapid recovery,' commented Steve.

'He must have had a first class nurse.'

'I did my best,' said Helen.

Steve raised his eyebrows at her.

'Are you going to the dance — now that your personal problems are less disheartening?'

'I hadn't thought about it.'

'But — almost the whole village will be there.'

'One hundred and thirty-five adults,' quoted Helen.

'Plus the survivors,' Steve reminded her.

Helen said, suddenly:

'Jim West asked me to go with him.'

Steve frowned and grunted.

'He did make a remarkable recovery.'

'Dr. Marsh will see him in the morning. He will say if he's recovered.'

'And if he is passed fit. Will you go to the dance with him?'

Helen bit her lip.

'I don't know . . . you expect me to go with you, don't you, Steve?'

'We usually go together — when Tommy isn't around.'

Helen said:

'I don't want to hurt anyone. So, I won't go.'

'That's silly,' protested Steve.

'If I turn you down and go with Jim — that will make you angry, and it will hurt Jim, if I go with you.'

'Does it matter, who takes who. Being there is the important thing,' reasoned Steve.

'Is that how you really feel, Steve?'

'Am I supposed to feel jealous or something — when I have lost you, already?'

'You have never shown jealousy, Steve. I suppose, that's because I was never the only woman in your life.'

'But, you are!' protested Steve.

Helen shook her head and said, with a smile:

'The lifeboat has always been your first love, Steve.'

'It is my job!' protested Steve.

'And your life,' Helen reminded him. 'I would do anything for you . . .'

'Steve — don't get me wrong. I am

'not jealous of your boat.'

'Is it that which has driven this wedge between us?'

'Of course not, Steve. I admire you for what you do.'

'That's alright then — because . . . '

'Yes, Steve?'

'I could never give up the lifeboat job for anyone. Not even you, Helen.'

'That's honest, Steve. I have come to realise that anyone who marries you will have to live with your job.'

Steve told her bluntly:

'You could do that, Helen. You have the courage.'

'I don't think I have,' she protested.

'These past couple of days has proved it. Ever since you believed that Tommy Carr was lost at sea, you have faced up to it. I haven't even seen you red-eyed.'

'The circumstances were unusual, Steve. There was so much here to worry about, besides personal loss.'

'You can use that as an excuse, Helen — but you will always be the woman for me.'

Helen thanked him for obtaining the good news for her, then she went outside. Steve stood in the doorway with her, while she slipped the hood of her coat over her head. The snow was falling heavily. Thick flakes that spat on the ground, and quickly turned to ice.

Helen glanced into Steve's face.

'I'll let you know about the dance,' she decided.

'Then, you might come?'

'I might.'

She trudged home. Jim wasn't where she had left him, and Miss Pegler was sitting in the chair he had vacated by the fire. A pair of candles feebly lit the room.

The retired nurse informed Helen that Jim had complained of a sore throat, and she had taken his temperature, then sent him back to bed.

'Too soon for him to be up and about,' she declared.

Helen looked glum.

'And, he spoke of going to the dance, tomorrow.'

'That's out of the question. He's weaker than he thinks.'

Miss Pegler gave Helen a curious look.

'Will you be going to the dance, Helen?'

'I can't make up my mind.'

'Hasn't Steve asked you?'

'Yes . . . '

'I am not sure the dance is a good thing.'

Helen registered her surprise.

'Why not. Everyone in the village must be terribly bored. They haven't seen outside the place for two days, now.'

'I smell trouble,' said Miss Pegler.

'You fear there will be a clash between the village boys and the survivors?'

'For one thing, there won't be enough lasses to go round. And, those that will be at the dance, are already spoken for. I can't see that stopping our visitors from muscling in.'

'I don't think the survivors are as bad as they have been painted. I agreed with everyone else that they got off on the wrong foot . . . but there is nothing wrong with Jim, and I'm sure the others are decent enough.'

'They seem to have found their way to the 'Tavern' by the noise they were kicking up,' commented Miss Pegler. 'It was quite early, but the singing and the swearing was loud enough for anyone passing to hear.'

Helen smiled, and assured the old nurse that she doubted if the men would get roaring drunk on the two pounds that had been allotted to them from the Seamen's Fund.

'They will be broke again, though,' concluded Miss Pegler.

The following morning, Dr. Marsh called to see Jim, and diagnosed the young man was suffering from a severe chill following his experience in the open boat, and when Helen peeped in to see him, she found Jim, far from well.

Miss Pegler volunteered to stay at home that evening and keep an eye on the patient, if Helen wanted to go to the dance.

Helen saw no reason why she shouldn't please Steve, and she called in at the lifeboat station to tell him of her decision.

He'd closed down the radio set a few minutes before, and because he still wore the headphones, it prompted Helen to ask if there was any more news about Tommy.

Steve had got nothing fresh to report, but the coastguard had confirmed that a messenger had been sent to Tommy's home to find out if he had returned from the continent, and to pass on a message from Helen that she was in good health and would get over to the headland town as soon as possible.

'Maybe, this evening your last remaining doubts about Tommy's safety will be lifted,' said Steve.

'That would put me in a terrific mood for the dance,' replied Helen.

They arranged a time when Steve should call for her. Everything else had been laid on. The three young men from the village who formed the trio — the pianist, who managed to tinkle his way through a variety of melodies on the ancient school piano, his brother who played a noisy accordian, and a cousin, who owned a set of drums.

There was to be tea and sandwiches served in the interval, while Judd, the caretaker was preparing the classroom for the evening's entertainment.

Helen could see the need for the dance as she walked back along the sea front to her cottage. The village was silent and deathlike.

The villagers had simply nothing to do to while away the time. Mostly, the snow kept them indoors, and when there was a lull, it was too freezingly cold to wander aimlessly from one end of the village to the other.

But, it was when darkness fell that tempers became frayed and patience ran out.

This evening would provide light relief to the harrowing situation of being snowbound for the third night in succession.

Everyone had an excuse to get dressed in their best and to attend the dance.

Helen was ready soon after tea, and sat in the front room, waiting for Steve.

When he was ten minutes late, she could not understand it. Steve was always punctual, unless he had been called to duty, and even when that happened, he would send word along to her.

At half-past seven, the time the dance was due to start, Steve had still not arrived.

Miss Pegler queried his absence, and then put forward the suggestion that perhaps Steve was hung up on that radio set in the station.

Helen waited no longer. More anxious than annoyed, she put on her coat and rubber boots, took her dancing shoes with her in a bag, and went along to discover the reason for Steve's delay.

The moment she approached the station, there felt something odd about the place.

Then, she saw that the back door that led to Steve's quarters was swinging open, and the solitary oil lamp was swaying in the wind.

Helen's pulse rate quickened and she burst into the small room. She grew cold with fright. Steve was sprawled across his table. The radio set had been smashed, and Helen could see there were things missing from the wall.

She trampled across a trail of broken glass. The room had been reduced to a shambles, and Helen had to hurl a chair out of her path before she could reach Steve.

She handled him gently, not knowing what to expect. He moaned when she touched his forehead. There was a tremendous bruise above his left eye, but he was breathing strongly, and there were no cuts on his face or head.

'Steve,' whispered Helen.

He started to come round, and the moaning grew louder. He clenched his fists and thumped them on the table, finally opening his eyes, and wincing when he became conscious of the pain.

'Who did this?' demanded Helen, with passion.

8

Helen pulled a chair to its feet, and helped Steve into it. He slumped in the seat, his head bowed.

Helen fussed over him, bathing the ugly swelling over his eye, but Steve put up with the treatment for barely a minute.

He pushed Helen's hand aside.

'No time for that.'

'Your eye will be closed, if . . . '

'God's sake, Helen. There maybe a couple of fanatics on the loose.'

Helen stood back from the injured man.

'It is no use rushing blindly off in pursuit. Can you remember anything?'

'I was on the radio . . . opening up, when I was attacked from behind. Someone pulled me round and I caught this fist in my eye.'

Helen expected Steve to be vague.

He was a big man, fully capable of handling most people who had a tendency towards blind aggression, and she was convinced that given half a chance, he would have held his attackers at bay. It was obvious, Steve never got that chance.

'Did you catch a glimpse . . . '

Steve shook his head.

'Not a thing.'

He climbed to his feet, and blew out his cheeks.

'I feel lousy,' he added.

'Take it easy, Steve.'

He leaned on the table for support, and he gasped aloud when he saw the smashed radio.

'It couldn't be worse,' he muttered.

'Our only link with Highport.'

'Now, we are completely isolated. Didn't they understand . . . '

'They?' queried Helen.

'Must have been more than one,' reasoned Steve. 'Someone acting alone wouldn't have licked me.'

'Why smash the radio?'

Steve fingered his bruises.

'Why do anything of this?'

He pushed his way through the débris, attempting to ascertain what was missing from his quarters. His glance fell upon the empty spaces on the wall, then back to Helen.

'This is damn serious,' he declared.

'What have they taken?'

Steve bit his lip.

'For a moment, I thought it was an act of senseless vandalism, but the Verey Pistols and the cartridges are missing.'

'Verey Pistols?'

'I use them for firing signals in the air.'

'Can they be used for anything else?'

'At short range — they could give anyone a nasty turn. But, in any case, the sight of a pistol could scare an innocent person.'

Helen looked straight at the destroyed radio set.

'This whole thing looks planned, Steve.'

He went over his movements that

evening, although he was impatient to get out after the thugs.

'I walked along to the school to make sure everything was ready for the dance. People had started turning up — villagers and survivors, together. Everyone seemed to be getting on well, and I stayed there until the dance kicked off . . . then I returned here, and hoped to get news about Tommy before meeting you.'

'When you left the school — was it packed?'

'I reckon it was almost full house.'

'I suppose you can't remember — who wasn't there?'

'I don't see . . . '

'Steve! Whoever planned this, intended doing it when everyone was at the dance. The village would be almost deserted down here on the sea front.'

Steve puckered his brow.

'I do remember having a count up to see if all the survivors had turned up. I especially wanted them there, so they could break the ice with the villagers.'

'Your dance could lead to disaster,' mused Helen.

Steve agreed with her.

'The thugs haven't taken all this trouble for kicks. They have a motive.'

He walked carefully to the door and announced:

'I'm ready to start searching.'

Helen restrained him again.

'Steve — they could have carried out what they intended doing, then calmly turned up at the dance afterwards.'

He narrowed his eyes.

'Is that why you asked if anyone was missing from the dance?'

Helen's glance darted round the room.

'We took a list of the survivors, and you gave the information over the radio. I remember writing the details in an exercise book.'

Steve nodded and turned back to the table. He tugged open the drawer, and retrieved the book. He scanned it, then gave up.

'My eyes are swimming. Here, you read it.'

Helen announced the names. She left out Jim West who was ill in bed, and the other sick survivor. Steve could account for all of the others being at the dance, except one — a burly youth named Stott.

'Only one,' murmured Helen. 'Could he have done this alone?'

'Wait a minute, Helen . . . who is Stott billeted with?'

'The Clegg family . . . '

Steve groaned. That was enough. The only flock of black sheep in the whole village.

'The Cleggs have always made trouble,' he said.

'Mrs. Clegg is in hospital,' recalled Helen.

'Her husband is in Maidstone prison,' added Steve. 'Who agreed to take in Stott?'

'An old aunt lives there. She's looking after the daughter.'

Steve grunted.

'Millie Clegg. She's a fast, empty-headed young lady.'

'I know Millie,' reflected Helen.

'She wasn't at the dance,' said Steve. 'She usually never misses.'

'Stott and Millie Clegg. They could make an explosive couple.'

'Sure, they could. Millie is tough and knows her way round the village, and I never liked the look of this fellow Stott.'

It was time to start looking. Steve stopped at the Clegg's cottage. The frail old aunt answered the door. She confirmed that both Millie and young Stott had gone out. To the dance, she believed.

It was a toss up whether to go straight to the school, and see if the young tearaways were there, or to scour the village to check if they had carried out any crime.

Steve decided to check on the village. The youngsters were armed. The telephones were dead. They could play havoc among the minute community who had not attended the dance.

'There is only the old folks, here,' he remarked.

The first evidence of a felony was at the home of Commander Forbes. His cottage was detached and stood on raised ground at one end of the sea front. The French windows that faced the Channel banged in the wind, and glass tinkled to the ground from a shattered frame.

Steve led the way in. Helen followed and then stood rooted to the carpet. She had experienced shock once tonight, now she was meeting it for the second time. From where she had halted, the retired Naval man looked badly hurt, and Helen's stomach turned over at the sight of blood staining the pale coloured carpet.

'See what you can do for him,' rapped Steve, without considering if Helen was in a fit state to attend to the casualty.

Steve ran from room to room, searching for the intruders, while Helen ventured closer to the unconscious Commander Forbes. She examined a head wound that was too deep for her to patch up, and her one aim at this stage was to make the poor man comfortable.

She collected a towel from the kitchen and a basin of water, then put a cushion under the man's head.

Steve roared grimly into the room.

'We need a doctor, here,' Helen told him, straightaway.

'And we need the police . . . there is a shotgun missing from the old man's library.'

'The constable is stranded outside the village with young Dr. Marsh,' murmured Helen.

'Those tearaways are really armed,' observed Steve, quietly.

He glanced down at Helen. They were in a bit of a fix. Steve had visions of the thugs, armed and reckless on the rampage in the village. He wanted to pick up their trail before they caused more damage and casualties, yet, he was gaining a strong suspicion that this was a well designed plan. He would have liked to have jumped ahead and forestalled the thugs reaching their ultimate target, but first things first.

'I'm going to call out Dr. Marsh,' announced Steve.

'The old boy will probably be in bed. He's got a rotten cold.'

'He'll turn out,' said Steve, confidently. 'Will you be alright?'

Helen was decidedly nervous, but she realised at this present time, nowhere in the village was safe while the tearaways were at large.

Armed, they could hold the village to ransom, and there was nothing anyone in Haven Bay could do about it. Surrounded by sea and snowdrifts, with a snowstorm raging overhead, and means of communication to the outside world now reduced to nothing, nobody was safe.

'You go and fetch the doctor — don't waste time,' replied Helen.

Steve strode to the door, then paused.

'It is unlikely they will pay this

cottage another visit. They got what they came for.'

Steve wanted more hands, but he would not risk allowing the elderly doctor to make his own way to the injured man's cottage. The doctor was valuable to the community, and if anything happened to him on the street, then matters would become incredibly difficult.

He returned with the doctor within fifteen minutes. Dr. Marsh took off his jacket and rolled up his sleeves, then as an added precaution, he took a service pistol from his jacket and laid it beside him. Then, he told Steve to get up to the school and stop the dancing.

'Enlist all the help you can. These thugs have got to be stopped.'

Steve went, and Helen stayed behind to assist the doctor. The injured man came round slowly as his wound was being cleansed.

Commander Forbes spoke frantically, but Dr. Marsh would not listen until he had got his job done.

'Don't get excited, Bill . . . I have to give you an injection, then I must put some stitches in that head wound.'

'I'll survive — get after them!' bellowed the Commander.

Because the doctor was too busy to listen, the retired Naval man clutched at Helen's sleeve.

'Be quiet,' whispered Helen.

Commander Forbes gripped the arms of the armchair where he had been placed for his treatment.

'Look up at the light,' instructed Dr. Marsh.

The light in the room was good. The Commander had salvaged some high pressure Tilley lamps from his service days, and put them to good use while the power was blacked-out in the village.

He managed to restrain himself until his wound was stitched, then with a brief thank you to his friend the doctor, he leaned forward in his chair and demanded attention.

'There was a time when you could

open your door to anyone in Haven Bay. Well, that's a myth now. I opened my door tonight to answer a knock, and before I knew what happened . . . '

'Have you got a headache, Bill?'

'Of course, I have, John . . . '

'Then stop raving on about what happened.'

Commander Forbes stared rebelliously at the doctor.

'This is important!'

'No more important than you getting some rest.'

Dr. Marsh took a chair opposite his patient.

'I'll stay and keep an eye on you.'

He looked thoughtfully at Helen.

'You had better scamper home, young lady — get behind a locked door and let the menfolk deal with this.'

'But, do you know who you are hunting for?' persisted Commander Forbes.

'We think so,' replied Helen.

'Well, I know 'em. I put up a fight, you see. There was that young rogue

Clegg's teenage daughter, and a hooligan with black hair smoothed back and evil eyes. Came in with the boatload of survivors, the other day.'

'We suspected as much,' said Helen.

'A dangerous couple,' added the Commander.

'They are armed,' Helen told him.

'Aye, the girl waved a Verey pistol in my face, while the hooligan started attacking me . . . '

'It is worse than that,' said Helen. 'They stole your shotgun.'

The Commander grew alarmed and he said curtly to Helen:

'Get off home, young woman.'

Helen glanced back at the two elderly gentlemen as she crossed the room. Dr. Marsh sat with his revolver in his lap trying to pacify the volatile Commander, while Bill Forbes shrugged huffily, bemoaning the fact that he wasn't twenty years younger.

Helen ploughed her way along the sea front. It was noisy with the smacking of the waves against the sea wall, and the wind howling along narrow alleyways between the cottages.

A sudden flurry of snow blinded her, and she could neither feel or see where she was going.

She ducked into one of the alleyways for shelter, and waited for the flurry to fade.

The alleyway led on to the High Street and was a short cut to the tiny row of village shops.

The snow was deep on the ground, but Helen could make out a solitary light burning from one of the shops. It cast a long, narrow shadow, and Helen detected that the shop door was open.

She glanced on the ground. There was a trench made by footsteps, revealing that the alleyway had just been used.

Helen made a rapid calculation. She counted the number of doors from the corner of the sea front, and came up with the unnerving conclusion, that the solitary light and the door, slightly open, belonged to the village Post Office.

9

The deep snow in the alleyway prevented Helen doing anything in a rush. Her approach to the Post Office was silent and slow.

She hesitated at the door that was ajar. Breathlessly, she pushed it, ready to shut her eyes if necessary.

The door widened, and the glow of the oil lamp in the centre of the small premises spotlighted a small, timid man bound and gagged, flopped in a tall backed chair and staring at the ceiling.

'Mr. Peters!' exclaimed Helen.

She shouldered her way in. The helpless postmaster could only just about stamp his feet in his excitement. Helen regarded the shadows that lurked in the shop with suspicion, but when she felt sure the intruders had fled, she swiftly went to the postmaster's aid.

The rope that had been used was

new and obviously stolen, probably from Steve's lifeboat shed, and it had bound the unfortunate man treacherously, blistering and cutting his hands, while sticking plaster smothered his mouth.

Helen acted as gently as she could, but the man was sorely shocked. Helen found some brandy in the back room of the shop, and gave Mr. Peters a swig of it.

His features took on a less frightening colour, and he sat there, wretchedly wringing his burning hands and trembling from the pains in his body.

'They took the lot,' he moaned.

It was a lot, too. Mr. Peters was holding more than a thousand pounds, that he had collected from Highport's general Post Office, four days ago. The cash was to cover the pay-out to customers, who drew on their deposits over the Christmas period. There was also the Christmas Club deposited by the 'Tavern' and a couple of Thrift Clubs run by local organisations.

'That Clegg family have been neighbours of mine for years,' protested Mr.
Peters.

'You recognised Millie, did you?'

'It was her right enough — and that
chap who 'as been living there.'

'Thank goodness you are not badly
hurt.'

'I might have been — but I did as
they asked the minute that lout stuck
that shotgun against my head.'

'You did right,' admitted Helen.

'They robbed me of everything they
lay their hands on. Tell you what, Miss
Foster — I reckon Millie Clegg
watched me carrying in the bags of
money, t'other morning. It stuck in her
mind ever since.'

'That's more than likely.'

'Bad streak runs in the family. She
was waiting for someone to turn up
who was ruthless enough to carry out
an armed robbery,' decided Mr. Peters.

'They planned the whole thing
together,' concluded Helen.

'But, where is it going to get them.

Maybe, they do have a thousand pounds in their pockets. How can they get out of the village.'

Mr. Peters was getting over his fright, and Helen decided she had to go and inform Steve that the young thugs had reached their ultimate objective.

'I feel a bit of a fool now that it is all over. Letting Millie inside, when she said her old aunt wasn't well. Never liked the Clegg family, but always tried to be a good neighbour.'

'You are not the only one who has been fooled tonight,' Helen told him.

She retreated to the door, and was about to remind the postmaster to make certain the door was bolted, when her glance detected a thin trail of blood.

She looked up at Mr. Peters.

'Are you sure you are unhurt?'

'Bit sore . . . but I wasn't treated too violently.'

'Someone has been losing blood!'

'That was the girl — she cut her wrist. Came in wi' it like that.'

Helen recalled the shattered window

on Commander Forbes' premises, and concluded that Millie could have been injured scrambling through the French windows.

'If I was a police dog I could probably trail them,' murmured Helen.

She left the little Post Office and Mr. Peters to do the clearing up, then instead of going home, headed for the school to meet Steve.

She was both puzzled and infuriated to hear music and laughter drifting out of the building as she approached, and she moved swiftly inside the school, taking in the enthusiastic scene at a glance.

Helen moved in among the dancers and became noticeable because of her unsuitable attire.

One young man did not care that she was in rubber boots, and he grabbed hold of Helen and whirled her round the floor.

'Stop this!' she cried.

'What's the trouble, Helen?'

'Where is Steve?'

She pulled herself out of the young man's arms. At a time like this, the music and the dancers behaviour appeared vulgar and callous. She snapped the question directly at her unwanted partner, and her intense manner caused him to frown.

'I haven't seen him, not since he got the dance under way.'

'He came up here — not long ago.'

The young man laughed.

'Bad luck, Helen — he's given you the slip.'

'Don't be ridiculous . . . '

'What's up with you?'

'Look — stop the music!'

'Eh!'

'We have got trouble in the village.'

She gave the young man a shove. He wandered in the direction of the trio who made the music, spoke to the pianist, and when the music ceased in the middle of a popular melody, the dancers protested with cat calls.

Helen raised her voice to be heard above the din.

'This is important. Has anyone seen Steve Day?'

It angered her to discover she was still not being taken seriously, and she was called a spoilsport for ruining the dance.

Helen decided to cut corners, and she yelled at them:

'The Post Office has been robbed!'

That was enough to gain their attention. The din became subdued, and questions were flung at Helen from all directions. She was upset because Steve had not reached the school to warn the villagers, and without his drive and leadership, chaos threatened to take over.

Helen put the facts to them. The radio set at the lifeboat station had been smashed. Commander Forbes was injured after putting up a fight against intruders, but they stole a shotgun and ammunition. Finally, Mr. Peters was bound and gagged while the thugs rifled the Post Office till. More than a thousand pounds had been stolen.

The dyed-in-the-wool villagers began

to criticise the newcomers to Haven Bay for the outrageous behaviour, and Helen saw the inevitable conflict begin to erupt between the locals and the survivors.

She killed the conflict by declaring that the attack on the innocents was a combined effort between a villager and a survivor.

One of the survivors spoke up:

'Then shouldn't we all get together and hunt 'em down, before they do more harm?'

There was a surge of people towards the door. Helen viewed them in the same way as if they were a mob. There was nobody to lead. Nobody to draw up a plan. Nobody to give orders. Just plain excitement as if this was some kind of adventure to relieve boredom.

'Wait!' cried Helen. 'This couple is armed.'

'They have nowhere to run to,' declared one of Steve's lifeboatmen.

'But, they still have to be found,' insisted Helen.

'Who are we looking for?' demanded the lifeboatman.

'A thug named Stott . . . '

''im!' said one of the survivors, with a growl. 'He's a nut case!'

'He's teamed up with Millie Clegg,' added Helen.

'Where were they last?'

'The Post Office.'

There was no stopping the mob, now. They trudged like an advancing column away from the school, and spread out along the High Street and the sea front, where they conducted a house to house search.

Helen feared something dreadful had happened to Steve, and when the search yielded no results, it was decided to call it off, and resume the hunt in daylight. It was obvious the couple were hiding up somewhere, but searching in the pitch black was a hopeless task, although all the calls made at the cottages were met with reassuring replies that the reckless couple had not been seen.

Helen disclosed her anxiety about Steve to old Judd, the caretaker, as he leaned on a stout stick that he had armed himself with.

'Steve came to warn the villagers at the school more than an hour ago. Now, he is missing.'

'We have called at every house in the village.'

'He was attacked by the thugs earlier . . . I wonder if he has suffered a reaction from the blow.'

'You mean, he could be wandering . . . '

'Not wandering, Mr. Judd. It is a dead end here on the sea front. He might be unconscious in some dark corner.'

'In this weather,' shuddered Judd.

Helen aimed a fearful glance at the spiteful sea.

'He could have fallen off the sea wall,' she whispered.

'Nothing tragic has happened to Steve. He's a man who likes to work alone. Maybe, he's following up some hunch.'

'That doesn't ring true, Mr. Judd. He was on his way to the school.'

'Ah! But, what if he caught a glimpse of the thugs, and gave chase?'

'There is no place to run to in Haven Bay — not while we are cut off by snowdrifts.'

The night was freezing and it was treacherous underfoot. The searchers dispersed, promising each other to join up again at daybreak. Then they went home and bolted doors and windows behind them.

Judd groped his way through the darkness, gripping his stick like a weapon as he headed for his cottage next to the school.

'Nothing like this ever happened in Haven Bay,' he had told Helen, just before they parted.

Helen covered the twenty yards to her lodgings. She glanced up at the bedroom windows, and saw a light filtering through from the back of the cottage.

She took out her key and unlocked

the front door. The Yale lock was released, but the door remained fast.

Helen assumed that Miss Pegler had bolted the door from the inside, upon advice from the men making the house to house call.

Helen rapped on the door. She heard footsteps advance along the hall.

'Who is that?' asked Miss Pegler, in a voice that was wary of danger.

'This is Helen.'

The bolt was drawn and the door prised open. A wafer of light pierced the darkness of the cold hall.

Then, Helen was hauled over the threshold and the door slammed in her wake.

It was the behaviour of a nervous, old lady.

Miss Pegler spoke tremulously:

'I'm sorry, Helen — they made me do it.'

Helen blinked into the darkness. Then a voice travelled down the stairs.

'Don't do anything silly. I'm standing at the top of the stairs, with a shotgun pointing at you.'

Helen stayed put until she was ordered otherwise. She asked the old nurse if she was all right.

'I have stopped shaking, Helen.'

'How did they get here?'

'They brought Steve . . . '

'Steve!'

'They held him up. Millie Clegg has cut her wrist, and I was forced to treat the wound.'

'Is Steve . . . '

'He's fine. It appears he's wanted for some crazy scheme this couple have devised. So, they won't harm him.'

'What about Jim?'

'He's too groggy to understand much what's going on.'

'How long have they been here?'

'Almost an hour.'

'When we were making house to house calls — couldn't anyone do anything?'

'Steve is tied to a chair upstairs, and I had a gun in my back. I had to tell the caller I was on my own except for the sick Jim.'

Stott swung a lamp into view. Helen stared up at him. The shotgun was tucked beneath his arm.

'Come on up — the pair o' you,' he snarled.

Helen went up the stairs, followed by Miss Pegler.

'Who are you?' demanded Stott.

He was big and beefy. Black hair and dark eyes. Aggressive and ruthless, without a lot of regard for danger. A vain, frivolous teenager like Millie Clegg would have been impressed by his swagger.

'Helen Foster — I live here.'

He menaced Miss Pegler with the gun.

'Is this the girl?'

'I told you I had a lodger.'

'No tricks, now . . . anyone else to come home?'

'Nobody else.'

Stott drew Helen towards him.

'You will make a pretty hostage.'

Helen stood stiff and erect, and averted her face from him.

'What is the point of all this?' she mumbled.

'I'll make myself clear — very soon,' he promised.

'You have stolen more than a thousand pounds, but you can't get out of this village.'

'I've got hostages,' Stott reminded her, 'and I've got a gun.'

10

Stott prodded Helen in the small of her back just to remind her that he was the man in charge of the situation.

She was pushed into her own room, where the beautifully developed blonde teenager, Millie Clegg sat on Helen's bed.

Millie was smoking, and held the loaded Verey pistol in her lap. She sneered at Helen, who she considered was too snooty by far, then she crossed her legs beneath the minute skirt, and said:

'Join the party!'

Helen stared past Stott's young moll at Steve, who was bound hand and foot and secured to a chair. Although he anticipated that sooner or later, Helen would walk into Stott's trap it didn't prevent him snapping in rage at Stott, who hovered in the doorway.

'You are trapped. Be sensible and give up this fool game.'

Stott leered at him.

'I'm safe.'

Stott scowled as Jim West's croaking cough from the small back room was loud enough to be heard through the thin walls. He signalled to Miss Pegler to go and attend to her patient, once more brandishing the shotgun in her face.

The old nurse didn't flinch. It had been a frightening experience at first when Stott and Millie had broken in and held her at gun point. Now, she had time for reflection. She had lived through a good and useful life, and she had precious little to lose at this stage.

The village had been outraged by these tearaways as if life wasn't difficult enough while the place was snow-bound. Miss Pegler was losing patience. She missed her friendly milkman's early morning call, and was tired of tinned milk. She had not been able to buy fresh fruit for three days. The postman hadn't called and it was no use writing letters for collection. There were no daily newspapers, and she missed the crossword in the *Telegraph*.

Above all, Christmas was just a week away and she had been invited over to Commander Forbes' home to share his turkey dinner with him.

She was angry that her fate should be left in the hands of this hooligan, who brought out the worst in her usually kindly nature.

Miss Pegler was also very shrewd. She could tell at a glance that Stott was being pestered by Millie Clegg. She had been useful to him, but that was nearly at an end now. It might upset the apple cart if Millie's position in the affair was made vulnerable.

'Didn't you hear what I said,' stormed Stott.

Everyone in the room grew tense as Miss Pegler defied the thug. Then suddenly, she looked past him, gave Millie a curious smile and wished the teenage girl a happy birthday.

'Silly old fool,' glowered Millie.

'Well, that's nice . . . ' murmured the old nurse. 'Is that all the thanks I get?'

'Thanks?' queried Millie, blushing, and absently dismissing a blonde curl from her eyes.

'For bringing you into the world. I remember the date and time, and the weather was like it is tonight. Close on midnight and fifteen years ago.'

Miss Pegler looked primly at Millie, and decided she had sown enough seeds of mistrust, then went into the small back room to give Jim a spoonful of linctus.

She smiled as she heard Stott raise his voice at Millie, and she reflected that she still had another card up her sleeve.

'Eighteen and a half you said you were!' Stott stormed at Millie.

'What does it matter?'

'Fifteen!' echoed Stott.

Helen exchanged a hopeful glance with Steve, then sat down at the foot of the bed to get a close view of the thieves falling out.

'I look more than eighteen,' protested Millie.

'You are under age.'

'And in need of care and protection,' murmured Steve.

Millie rounded on him.

'Shut up you. I've got a score to settle . . . '

'You'll leave him alone,' drawled Stott.

'He gave evidence that put my old man in prison.'

'Anyone stealing emergency rations from a boat on the sea wall deserves all he gets,' reflected Steve, grimly.

Millie spun round and faced Stott.

'Is that all you're going to do. Stand there, while he insults me.'

'Get lost,' snarled Stott.

'You said we were going to get married. You promised,' wailed Millie.

'I didn't know you were fifteen, then.'

'Don't be mean . . . '

'Listen,' said Stott. 'I'll take my chances with a robbery rap, but I am not sticking my neck out for an abduction. You get short shift in prison from the other guys when you mess about with young girls.'

'Aren't you taking me with you?' whimpered Millie.

Stott sniffed.

'Get in the next room and tell the old lady to make some tea . . . and don't let her out of your sight. She's too smart for my liking.'

Millie slid off the bed, and flashing Stott a glance that was a mixture of fear and contempt, she went to enforce her authority on Miss Pegler.

As the door of the next room opened, Jim's awful cough seemed to fill the cottage.

'That guy gets on my nerves,' declared Stott.

'You haven't a chance,' Steve warned him.

'Four hostages will be enough.'

'The odds are growing less,' retorted Steve. 'You can't rely on Millie — not now.'

Helen said:

'Send the girl to her home. She shouldn't be mixed up in this.'

'Do you think I am mad?'

Helen thought he was, but she didn't tell him to his face.

'It will be one against five by the morning,' she observed 'Just mark my words.'

Stott snorted at her. He was eight years over twenty, and all but six weeks of those eight years had been spent on three separate prison sentences. But, he congratulated himself that he learned by his mistakes, and when he devised the plan of robbing the village postmaster, he knew that he would have to get rid of the only remaining link between Haven Bay and Highport. He knew that Steve's radio messages could not bring immediate help while the village was snowbound, but he could tell the outside world what was taking place, and that was warning enough to reduce the time he needed to get away.

Stott stroked his chin and stared at

Steve. The lifeboatman was worried about the state of his beloved village. People had been hurt tonight, and it was a matter of pride to put things right, while he was in charge.

Steve wondered what was happening outside. He had heard the advancing footsteps when the house to house call was being carried out, and he suffered frustration when the footsteps receded.

He was convinced that everyone in the cottage was in danger, and he shared Helen's opinion that Stott was crazy.

'Why are you holding us?' Steve demanded.

Stott gave him a questioning look.

'You don't believe I can get out of this village, do you?'

'It is impossible.'

'Nothing is impossible to a desperate man.'

'Haven Bay is cut off, and unless the weather suddenly improves we will remain snowbound for a couple more days yet. The snow ploughs are not getting through . . . '

Stott giggled oddly.

'You are talking about overland.'

Steve held his breath, and suddenly, he realised why he was being held prisoner. It added up, why Stott wanted hostages, too.

'You are not serious — surely?'

Stott held his face close to Steve. Helen was convinced if Steve hadn't been tied, he would have delivered the thug a blow that would have carried him to the far corner of the room.

'Damn serious, mate!'

'Do you imagine in your wildest dreams — that you can leave this village by boat?'

'I ain't dreaming.'

'There has been a blizzard blowing along the Straits for three days now without a let-up. Nobody could launch a boat . . . '

'You did,' challenged Stott.

'The lifeboat, maybe . . . '

'That's what I mean. The lifeboat!'

Helen shook her head in dismay. It

was the craziest of schemes, yet, Stott had faith in his planning.

'You mean — launch the lifeboat, so that you can escape from this village.'

'Why not. You rescued a boatload of survivors when the blizzard was raging?'

'To bring them ashore here. Where do you plan to go?'

Stott grew intent.

'I got the idea by looking at my passport. It's got a couple of months to run before it expires.'

Steve was wondering what the fool was going to suggest next.

'Are you suggesting that I should take the lifeboat across the Channel — with you aboard?'

'Nothing as hazardous as that. But, you could ship me across the bay to the headland. Roughly six miles, ain't it?'

Steve drew a deep breath.

'You reckon you have got it figured?'

'I reckon so. I have a time-table of the ferry departures. There is one leaving Highport, tomorrow evening. I aim to be in Highport in time to be on that ferry — two hours later I'll get off in Ostend, then vanish!'

'It won't work, Stott.'

'You are bluffing. I heard it said in the village a couple days back, that if conditions here got worse, you would take the lifeboat across the bay to Highport.'

'I'd risk my neck fetching essential supplies for the village, but not to help you escape.'

'If you won't risk your neck,' Stott warned him. 'Then, you will be risking the pretty neck of this young lady.'

Stott brought the gun up and aimed it at Helen's throat. Steve gritted his teeth.

'You won't get away with it. Too many obstacles.'

Stott was convinced that the lifeboat-man's tone was less positive, and he had real hope of getting some co-operation.

'Name me an obstacle,' he challenged.

'The obvious one is that I have to have my crew. I can't handle the lifeboat on my own.'

'You will have your crew. In fact, it will be the trip to collect essential supplies that you proposed to take. The one difference being — is that I will be aboard.'

'You forget, I'm in charge of the village. Everyone depends on me to arrange things. Such a trip will take all day to arrange.'

'I understand that.'

'Then — how . . . when I'm your prisoner?'

'I intend releasing you.'

Steve gave Helen a swift glance. It was brutally apparent where the hostages came in.

Stott would hold them in the cottage, while Steve made the arrangements to get the lifeboat ship-shape for the trip to the headland.

If he spoke out of turn, or did anything to arouse the villagers' suspicions and ruin the thug's plan, then the consequences were too horrible to consider.

'I don't believe you can trust me, Stott?'

'I can trust you not to do anything reckless.'

Steve thought of Helen, and dear Miss Pegler, even the groggy Jim West were under threat of death.

'Is it worth that paltry sum you robbed . . . '

'I ain't ever laid hands on a thousand quid before. That ain't paltry to me.'

'A safe conduct out of Haven Bay,' mused Steve.

'Is it a deal?'

Helen stormed at him before Steve could reply.

'You could never shoot all of us, if Steve disclosed . . . '

'I'm banking on Steve — not wanting anyone killed,' retorted Stott.

Steve nodded cautiously.

'I'll do it.'

'Great.'

'When do I get out of these ropes?'

Stott held up the shotgun and signalled for Helen to untie Steve. Then he backed to the door.

'I'll be back to discuss details — right now, I want a cup of tea, but remember, Millie will be right outside this door, just in case you break out . . . and that girl, really hates you, Steve!'

He locked the couple in the room. Steve rubbed his hands to get the circulation moving, while Helen sat on the bed, staring numbly at the framed photograph of Tommy, on the bedside table.

He seemed to be getting farther and farther away from her all of the time.

Steve caught her studying the photograph.

'I suppose — this could be a blessing in disguise, Helen.'

She could not see how an armed thug with crazy notions could be called a blessing in any sense of the word.

'How do you work that out?'

'If I'm being forced to take the lifeboat across the bay to Highport, then I can find out what's happened to Tommy.'

'Poor Tommy,' murmured Helen. 'He must be at his wit's end.'

'This nightmare may soon be over.'

'But, Steve — it is wrong. All wrong to help this thug escape ... I can't forget the shock I had seeing you out cold on the floor, and then poor Commander Forbes.'

Steve stretched out on the bed.

'I'm whacked — and I reckon we are in for an eventful twenty-four hours,' he concluded.

11

Helen turned her head and pondered over Steve as he tried to sleep. The swelling over his left eye looked painful, and she guessed his head still ached from the coshing he had received. She felt deeply concerned for his well-being, and as her glance took in the photograph of the stylish Tommy Carr, she was reminded of the problem that never left her all the while the two men claimed to love her.

She knew her affection for Steve went very deep, and this sudden closeness in this gloomy bedroom, facing together what must be the biggest crisis of their lives, made her think again about the part he played in her life.

Helen felt incredibly comfortable all the time Steve was with her. Even when he was bound to the chair earlier on, helpless to raise a finger to assist her, she dismissed her fear, simply because he was a captive as well.

Yet, she had to admit, Tommy's presence also gave her comfort, and indeed something more. He infected her with excitement. Tommy had dash and exuberance. He took chances over everyday living, while Steve was stolid, and in his dangerous job, he seemed to accept the risks with a cold calculating eye, refusing to blunder into anything without knowing what his chances of success were.

It seemed odd, that a smart young operator of a travel agency should appeal more romantically to her, than did the rugged chief of the local lifeboat. But, Helen had stopped trying to reason with her innermost feelings. They were there, and what she felt for Tommy didn't exactly happen when she was with Steve. He had been such a wonderful friend from the first day she had arrived in Haven Bay, but he had never swept her off her feet, and she continued to treat him as a friend. If they differed about the kind of feelings they had for each other, Helen was convinced that Steve would never let her down, no matter what the situation.

But, her feelings for Tommy were romantic and they were never more positive than when she first feared he was missing from the sunk ferry. It was not until she received the news that nobody aboard the ferry had perished was she able to revert to less passionate thoughts about him.

She sat on the edge of the bed, with the feeble light from the oil lamp tossing weird shadows from wall to wall, and gave consideration to the past few days of high drama.

It had such an ordinary beginning. She had closed the school after the children's Christmas party and left the village to meet Tommy as he embarked from the ferry at Highport.

But, the first of the blizzards, a storm ravaged sea, the launching of the lifeboat and the rescuing of twenty-two rather undesirable survivors, giving them shelter in the snowbound village, changed all that. Helen never got to Highport, that evening, and along with the rest of the locals she was doomed to remain snowbound while the treacherous winds stayed trapped in the hills beyond Haven Bay.

Even so, those events were almost tame compared to the present situation . . .

Steve stirred beside her, and Helen just managed to perceive that his eyes were open.

'I thought you were asleep,' said Helen.

'I wanted to,' admitted Steve.

'The situation hardly encourages peace of mind,' said Helen.

'I have been thinking.'

'What about?'

'The chances of escaping.'

'Steve — someone could get killed,' protested Helen.

'I know . . . but isn't it maddening. All of us in this cottage, no way out of the village, and yet we are prisoners. If we could attract attention!'

'Stott is lurking somewhere with that beastly gun. I am sure he will use it and defy the consequences if anyone from outside interferes.'

'If it was just me — I wouldn't hesitate taking a risk,' said Steve.

'Why should you?'

'I feel responsible.'

'You!'

'I took charge of the village because the police constable was away . . . '

'You organised the comfort of the survivors, and did it well, Steve. How were you to know that a ruthless little thug would rise out of that boatload of men?'

'I realise I could not anticipate that. But, I should have stopped him.'

'Stott has power in his hands. That is the reason why you couldn't prevent him running wild through the village.'

There was a brief pause.

'Steve,' murmured Helen. 'What are your chances of getting across the bay in this weather?'

'I have put to sea in worse conditions.'

'For an honest cause, maybe.'

'I hate the idea of the trip — just to give Stott safe conduct to the headland, but I am responsible for the safety of the people in this cottage. Stott has forced my hand.'

'Won't you be putting the lives of your crew at risk?'

Steve looked at her, sharply.

'My men won't question my decision.'

'Will you tell them the real reason for the trip?'

'Stott hasn't outlined his plan yet. I will know what I can or can't do, later on.'

'You ought to sleep, Steve. Tomorrow will be a tough day.'

'What about you?'

'I don't have to face the prospect of taking a lifeboat out in this arctic weather.'

'It will be pretty tense for everyone in this cottage after daybreak. Stott has got to bluff his way through another day before he gets out of this village.'

'Are you thinking of stopping him, Steve?'

'Not at the moment . . . get some rest, Helen.'

She kicked off her shoes and swung her legs up on the bed. They lay side by side, without touching, until Steve felt Helen shiver violently.

Without a word he put out his arm and pulled her closer, then said quietly:

'Go to sleep.'

She slept perfectly and did not stir until she heard the snow thudding against the window and someone was advancing along the passage.

The footsteps stopped outside the bedroom door, and Helen shot upright, as if guilty of being discovered in Steve's arms.

She was on her feet and waiting for the caller, seconds before Millie entered.

The blonde teenager raised her eyebrows at the crumpled bedclothes, and at Steve, still fast asleep.

'Cosy,' she murmured.

'Try knocking for a change,' retorted Helen.

Millie pointed at Steve.

'He's to go downstairs — now.'

'Stott's orders, I suppose?'

'Who else?'

Helen gave the girl a close look. Millie was in a foul mood, and the elation of yesterday when she was over the moon with the prospects of a runaway marriage with Stott, appeared to have vanished.

'I'll wake him,' said Helen.

She aroused Steve. He too had slept warmly and soundly, and the couple regarded each other with even greater respect, than they previously had.

'Good morning,' he greeted her, cheerfully.

'Steve . . . '

He put out his hand and touched her cheek.

'There isn't a soul in this world who would believe what happened between us, last night.'

'Nothing happened,' whispered Helen.

'That's right,' grinned Steve.

'Of course . . . we trust each other.'

Steve gave her a kind look.

160

'I have never loved anyone . . . '

'What's come over you, Steve?'

'Nothing, that I don't think was there all of the time.'

'Stott is waiting. Don't make him sore.'

'Let him wait . . . I figure that he needs me, more than I need him in this deal.'

'Be careful — you are in a fighting mood, Steve.'

'That's right, Helen. I'm fighting all of the way from now on.'

He jumped off the bed, and before striding to the door, he added:

'And, you are included in my fight.'

'What do you mean?'

'Tommy Carr hasn't won you, yet.'

Steve went out of the room as if he was going to eat Stott for breakfast, while Millie lingered behind uncertainly.

Helen swished open the curtains and rubbed her arms impulsively as she took in the cold weather that attacked the deserted sea front.

She was not aware that Millie was nosing round the room, until she heard a movement behind her.

Helen swung round, and caught Millie handling Tommy's photograph.

'Please, put that down,' requested Helen.

Millie sniffed. She was rebellious towards Helen. She loathed the quiet village. She had an intense dislike towards Steve. She resented the proud and particular Miss Pegler, but the choice was suddenly open to her to change sides. She wanted revenge on Stott, who had used her shamefully and was on the verge of dropping her like an empty paper bag.

The couple had spent the night quarrelling and bargaining. Stott agreed to take Millie as far as Highport and that was the limit. He would hand over two hundred pounds from the loot, so that she could get to another town and not have to face the wrath of Haven Bay's respectable residents.

Millie wanted a larger share if she was to be deserted. After all, there would never have been a robbery if she hadn't tipped Stott off about Mr. Peters taking the money into his post office, and it was her suggestion that they break into Commander Forbes' cottage and steal his shotgun. She had seen it there, when she had gone to the cottage to help her mother do some spring cleaning for the man.

She didn't quite know how to approach Helen, and after commenting that it was a nice photograph of Tommy Carr, she replaced it.

Helen gave the girl a puzzled stare.

'You know Tommy?'

'I recognised him by the photograph.'

'You have seen him in the village?'

'No.'

Helen wondered how Millie had recognised Tommy so readily by his photograph, if she had not actually seen them together.

'Somewhere else then? I admit, Tommy has only called for me at Haven

Bay a couple of times. Highport has been our 'scene'.'

'I ain't ever seen you wi' Tommy Carr,' admitted Millie.

Helen grew cautious. So that's the game. The teenager certainly was a cunning and spiteful little vixen.

'Stop being vindictive, Millie . . . '

'I'm not,' protested Millie, almost politely.

'Why are you trying to stir trouble?'

'Don't get huffy . . . I only recognised Tommy.'

'You spoke as if you — knew him?'

'Well, I do!'

'You know he runs a Travel Agency in Highport. Is that it?'

'He told me that,' admitted Millie.

Helen refused to be teased, but she was forced to conclude that this strange conversation was only inspired by Millie's recognition of Tommy's photograph.

'What are you trying to tell me, Millie?'

Millie put on an injured expression.

'Nothing at all. I made a remark about the photograph. Why are you so jumpy?'

Helen bit her lip. She was going to face facts for the first time. She had been desperate to meet Tommy at Highport when the ferry docked, because she had suspected an indifference in him of late that was difficult to ignore. Tommy had insisted that everything was fine. He loved her. The business was thriving, and if he appeared cool towards her, then it just had to be her own imagination playing tricks.

Suddenly, because of a third party, Helen made no attempt to quell the suspicions that were forming in her mind.

'I wish you would stop wasting time and explain,' challenged Helen.

'On Monday I went to see my mother in hospital. I missed the bus back to Highport, and Tommy gave me a lift. It had been a long cold journey from Canterbury, so when we got to

Highport, Tommy bought me a coffee.'

'And you talked?'

'Yes, we talked.'

'Did he mention me?'

'No, just where he worked . . . in fact, I got the impression that he was trying to pick me up.'

'You are an awful little liar,' stormed Helen.

'I am not!'

'I happen to know that Tommy left Highport, early Monday morning for Paris. So he couldn't have given you a lift, that evening.'

Millie pointed at the photograph on Helen's bedside table.

'That is the man I met on Monday night.'

'Go away . . . go back to your gangster friend.'

Millie shook her head in genuine dismay.

'I dunno — you can't win, can you.'

'What does that remark mean?'

'I wanted to talk to you — private like. I had no intention of upsetting you over a mouldy, old photograph.'

Helen sank on to the bed. Her face was pink with confusion.

'You can talk,' she invited.

'I ain't going along wi' friend Stott. He's let me down.'

Helen looked up curtly.

'You want to come over on our side?'

'As long as he doesn't know.'

'I don't know if I can trust you,' said Helen.

12

Helen had no time to accept Millie's offer. Jim West awoke in the small back room with a fit of coughing, and as Miss Pegler was downstairs in the kitchen, trying to rustle up some breakfast for Stott, she went to him immediately.

Helen gave Jim some of the linctus that Dr. Marsh had left for him on his last call, and once the irritation in his throat had dispersed, Jim seemed much better. He had slept throughout most of the night, but was rather vague about the present situation.

'We seem to have a crowd here, all of a sudden, Helen . . . people coming and going — what's it all about?'

Helen saw no point in hiding the truth from the sick young man.

'We are being held hostage, Jim.'

'What!'

'Sounds crazy, I know.'

'Is the village still snowbound?'

'Yes.'

'Then, how in the name . . . who is doing this, Helen?'

'One of the survivors — Stott, together with Millie Clegg. She's a local bad 'un.'

'Why are we hostages?'

'Stott and Millie robbed the village postmaster of a thousand pounds, and took over the cottage.'

'Is Miss Pegler safe?'

The old nurse had obviously won the young man's affection. His expression became anxious until Helen assured him that Miss Pegler was proving more than a match for the thug.

'She's fine, and already managed to drive a wedge between Stott and Millie.'

'But, what is the sense of robbing anyone. If it had been a million — they can't escape.'

'Stott is convinced he can get out of the village.'

'With the roads blocked?'

'He is holding Steve, as well . . . he's planning to reach Highport by boat across the bay. It is about a six-mile trip.'

'The man's a maniac!' stormed Jim.

He pulled himself up on the pillows, and asked Helen to hand him his clothes.

'I'll go and talk to Stott. After all, we were in the same tourist party.'

Helen refused to hand over the clothes and gently pushed Jim down into the bed.

'Keep warm — you got up too soon before.'

Jim gave a rueful smile.

'I asked you to go to the village dance, with me.'

'That dance was a lot of bother. While the village was almost deserted, Stott and Millie began their terrorising campaign.'

Jim squeezed Helen's hand.

'I feel pretty good, this morning. Let me handle Stott.'

'You don't understand. He is armed — otherwise I don't think he would last ten seconds against Steve.'

'I imagined he was armed,' admitted Jim. 'But, I have nothing to lose, Helen.'

'What are you talking about!' Helen rapped him smartly. 'Of course you have as much to lose as anyone of us.'

'Have you forgotten I'm a loser?'

'Just a crisis in your life. I am facing one too.'

'My wife's in Belgium with another man. Is that just a crisis?'

'Risking your life at the hands of a gunman isn't going to help.'

'Are we going to let Stott get away with this?'

'Steve reckons it isn't the time for heroics,' then she added: 'Now, just you lie still and I'll see what the chances are for breakfast.'

Helen slipped out of his room, and met Steve on the landing.

'Millie passed me on the stairs — with a face like thunder,' he recalled.

'She suggested she come over to our side. She's fallen out with Stott.'

Steve ushered her into the bedroom.

'What did you tell her?'

'That I didn't think I could trust her.'

'Just as well,' murmured Steve.

Helen sat on the bed. Steve took the chair by the window. The morning was white. The snow and winds unrelenting. He could see no farther than the sea wall, but knew that the waves were high in the Channel by the way the little cottage shuddered.

'I suppose Millie would have meant one more for Stott to keep watch over,' remarked Helen.

'He wouldn't worry about that. One hostage is always in danger while he holds that gun. That is enough to make anyone think twice before trying to win a medal.'

'Jim West offered to go and reason with him. They know each other slightly.'

'Jim might be more help later, when he's got his strength back.'

'What is happening downstairs, now?'

'Stott is standing over Miss Pegler, while she cooks breakfast for him. He's got the idea she might try and poison him.'

'I believe he really is afraid of the old nurse.'

'She makes him feel confused. That business about Millie being under age hit him like a rocket.'

'Any chance of breakfast for the rest of us?' asked Helen.

'I don't think so. There isn't much food in Miss Pegler's larder, and Stott figures on getting us down.'

'Jim ought to have something. He's pretty weak after the fever.'

'The smell of cooking made my mouth water,' confessed Steve.

'If Stott expects you to take the lifeboat out in this weather, surely he will have the decency to let you have a meal.'

Steve smiled grimly.

'Decency?' he queried. 'That thug hasn't heard of the word.'

'What can we do?' implored Helen.

Steve took her hands.

'Do as Stott tells you. Promise me that. It is going to be very delicate here, today.'

'Has he outlined his plan, then?'

'Yes,' replied Steve, gravely.

'I suspected as much.'

'He is more crazy than I first thought.'

'What is likely to happen?'

Steve told her. He was to act as go-between. The villagers, every person in Haven Bay was to be assembled and warned that Stott was holding some of the residents hostage.

The lifeboat crew with Steve at the helm of the boat and taking on Stott as a passenger would leave for Highport by late afternoon.

He had no fear of his plan being given away in advance to the outside world, because the village was cut off.

'That is why he destroyed the radio set,' observed Helen.

'He's thought it all out from A to Z,'

confirmed Steve.

'But, he's still got to get through the barrier at Highport to go aboard the ferry,' queried Helen.

'He has realised that, my love . . . that is why he intends taking you with him.'

'Me — why!'

'He searched every room in this cottage before you got home, last night. He came across your passport, Helen.'

'And, that has given him an idea — since he now refuses to take Millie?'

'He considers you are more mature to be seen making the trip with him.'

'I shall refuse to go,' insisted Helen.

'Helen — I want you to do as you are told. Leave the action to me. I promise you I will come up with something.'

'You mean — you will land Stott and myself at Highport, and just depart again. Won't you warn anyone, so that he can be stopped!'

Steve sighed because Helen was being difficult.

'He not only found your passport,

Helen. He showed me a wicked looking knife he found among Miss Pegler's kitchenware. He promised me, that he would be holding this knife, very close to you — all the way to Ostend. I refuse to bargain your life for . . . '

'Good God, Steve — he has thought of everything.'

'It wouldn't work unless we were snowbound. That is where Stott is safe. He's got the only gun in the village. Nobody can get a message out, and no villager is going to see one of their friends shot.'

Steve glanced away from Helen and out of the window.

'What wouldn't I give for a glimpse of the sun and blue sky. If only this snow would start to thaw.'

He stood up and said he would have to leave. He had to warn the villagers what was taking place. Helen recalled that another search was going to start at daybreak. If anyone made a clumsy move, it could mean disaster.

Steve hesitated, then leaned forward

and kissed Helen, lightly on the lips.

'I am sorry you have to carry such a huge burden,' he told her.

'No more than you, Steve.'

'I was thinking about Tommy . . . '

Helen averted her eyes from him and chewed her lip. She nodded dismally.

'My sole aim, ever since Haven Bay became snowbound was to get out of this village at the earliest opportunity to meet Tommy.'

'Now, it appears that you will be whisked across the Channel with a thug. I promise you, Helen . . . '

She stopped him abruptly.

'I can't be sure about Tommy, anymore.'

Steve frowned.

'What's that?'

'Millie told me that Tommy picked her up in Canterbury on Monday night, and drove her across to Highport.'

'She's spinning you a yarn out of sheer spite,' said Steve. 'I can see why you couldn't trust her.'

'If only I could be certain . . . '

'You told me Tommy was in Paris on Monday!'

'Tommy told me that. We arranged to meet off the ferry, the next day.'

'But, he wasn't on board when the ferry went down,' queried Steve. 'And he was not among the survivors.'

'So, if Millie spoke the truth, Tommy had no need to get aboard the ferry at Ostend — because he was already over here, and he never left Highport.'

'What's his game?' demanded Steve, angrily.

'It adds up, that Tommy never intended meeting me. Yet, I telephoned his parents the night the ferry went down, and they 'thought' he was one of the passengers.'

'Why the mystery?'

'I don't know.'

'But, you were left eating out your heart over him. His parents were worried stiff, and all the while, he was runing around in his car, picking up a fifteen-year-old.'

'Only, if Millie was telling the truth,'

said Helen, hopefully.

'Are you likely to get the truth from her?'

'I doubt it. If I start asking questions, she'll play on my curiosity,' said Helen.

'I reckon it is important for you to get over to Highport,' decided Steve.

'I can't live in doubt, Steve. Honesty has always been important to me.'

Steve held her in his arms and spoke frankly:

'Be patient, love. I am no hypocrite and I won't say I'm sorry if Tommy Carr has let you down. I'll be angry because he's given you an anxious time, and maybe I'll want to punch his head for telling you lies, but I want to know the truth, too — more so, than ever before.'

He kissed her again, with more seriousness linked to it, and Helen found she was able to return the kiss. It was as if she had made up her mind to believe Millie Clegg.

'I must go,' he said.

'You be careful,' said Helen.

'The locals are going to be sick about this,' commented Steve.

He had got as far as the door when a scuffling in the snow from outside the cottage caused him to glance back.

'Is that someone coming here?' he asked.

Helen was already at the window.

'It is Dr. Marsh!'

Steve widened his eyes.

'He's called to see Jim West . . . but, this early!'

'I expect he came straight from Commander Forbes' place. He stayed with the old chap after the break-in, last night.'

'I better get downstairs. Must avoid trouble,' said Steve.

Then, Helen remembered something about last night that coupled itself with a remark that Steve had made earlier concerning Stott possessing the only gun in the village.

'Steve!'

She clattered downstairs after him,

and clutched at his sleeve.

'What's up?'

'Dr. Marsh is probably carrying a pistol.'

'How . . . '

'He had it with him, last night — remember?'

'I do now,' admitted Steve, solemnly. 'He picked it up when I went to call him out to examine the Commander.'

'The doctor will stand no nonsense — and if Stott threatens him . . . '

Steve carried on downstairs.

'We dare not risk a gun battle. Because, that's likely to happen.'

Helen arrived at the foot of the stairs, close behind Steve. The knock on the front door brought Stott to his feet. He'd been eating fried bacon with four day old bread toasted. Miss Pegler had made it up into a sandwich for him, so that he had one hand on his gun.

Miss Pegler looked amused. This was the other trump card she had up her sleeve. Better than the one she had played against Stott when she informed him of Millie's true age.

'Nobody move,' snapped Stott, and took up a firing position in the hall.

13

Dr. Marsh knocked on the door again, and there was a moment of indecision from Stott.

Miss Pegler knew that the elderly doctor was going to call to visit the sick Jim West. She banked on this element of surprise, fully aware that the gunman could not have his eyes everywhere at once.

She glanced at Steve, convinced he was the man to make a dive at the thug.

Helen trembled at the thought of the door being opened and two men, both armed facing each other.

Millie Clegg chewed at her fingers. The excitement and adventure she had gained from her association with Stott had vanished. She had no desire to see any of the people she lived among hurt.

Stott rounded upon Miss Pegler. His features looked savage.

'Who is it?'

'The doctor has called to see Jim.'

'Send him away.'

'The lad upstairs needs a doctor. I want him to come in.'

Steve began to sweat. He realised that the old nurse was taunting the gunman too far, and more important, she did not know that Dr. Marsh possessed a pistol.

'The doctor will know soon enough what is going on,' said Steve. 'Let me open the door to him . . . you can cover me with your gun.'

Miss Pegler was tragically disappointed with Steve's offer. She was convinced that appeasement was not the answer. Sacrifices must be made if this thug was to be stopped terrorising the peace-loving and humble community.

Her lively imagination that saw a short scuffle with Stott, with him being overpowered, and sat on, was no longer so vivid.

Now, the element of surprise was

lost, and the gunman would gain the upper hand, once more.

Dr. Marsh's knock on the door became impatient, and he lent his gruff, cold-affected voice to his summons.

'Anyone at home!'

'Get rid of him,' Stott ordered Miss Pegler.

The old nurse thought swiftly. Not all was lost. The doctor was a sensible and determined man. If he got some kind of warning, then he would certainly do something about the gunman that held them hostage.

Helen tried to catch Miss Pegler's eye, without giving the game away that Dr. Marsh was armed, but the old nurse seemed to think she was playing a lone hand.

She marched into the hall. Stott behaved warily, moving back into the room, and holding the gun close to Helen.

'No tricks,' he snarled.

Steve clenched his fists and roared at Stott.

'I made you an offer . . . leave Helen alone.'

The moment took an ugly turn, as Steve moved forward.

'Stay put,' rapped Stott.

Steve kept coming. Helen froze. She was close enough to Stott to see him playing the trigger of the shotgun.

'Going to shoot me, Stott?' challenged Steve.

'I'll shoot your girl.'

'If you shoot anyone you are finished.'

'I am not bluffing,' the gunman warned Steve.

'Neither am I . . . you need me to get you out of this village.'

Suddenly, help came from an unexpected quarter. Millie grabbed Helen from behind and pulled her away, and before Stott realised what had happened, Steve put himself between the gunman and the girl.

Miss Pegler acted too, convinced all along that Steve had good, red blood flowing in his veins.

She opened the flap of the letter box and shouted at the doctor.

'We are held here by that young thug . . . warn the village!'

The doctor was annoyingly concerned for a second.

'Miss Pegler are you alright?'

'Yes — get help!'

The doctor made himself mobile despite his aching, old bones and the deep snow.

Miss Pegler turned and faced the savage young thug.

'I got rid of him,' she told him, almost sweetly.

Stott was white-faced, breathless and suffering from an attack of nerves. He hadn't fired at Steve because just in time, he realised that his plan of escape wouldn't work if he didn't have the coxswain of the local lifeboat to transport him across the bay.

The success of his robbery was only second importance to that of seeing his escape through. It pleased his ego that he could take over an entire village, and watch them regard him helplessly as he got away.

He had to have Steve to make the plan succeed, and what if the villagers were warned in advance where he was, the situation had not changed.

'You took a risk there, chum,' he told Steve.

'We've got a deal,' Steve reminded him. 'I'll give you safe conduct out of the village. You agree that nobody gets hurt.'

Stott nodded.

'That's the deal — but you see that everyone behaves themselves.'

He slunk to a corner of the room, giving Millie a violent slap in the face as he passed her.

Helen picked up the girl as she fell to the floor.

'Get her out of my sight,' he ordered.

Stott sat with the gun pointing at Miss Pegler.

'You stay down here with me.'

He directed Steve to go out and warn the villagers not to do anything silly that might cause bloodshed.

Helen smiled at him as she took Millie upstairs out of Stott's way.

The cottage door banged as Steve stepped out on to the sea front, while Helen and Millie took refuge in the bedroom.

Helen said:

'You risked your neck to get me out of a nasty situation. Thank you.'

Millie fingered her sore face.

'I wanted to come over on your side.'

'Sorry, I told you I couldn't trust you.'

'It was honest,' said Millie, humbly. 'So, I had to prove I was sincere.'

'If only you had been sincere . . . ' began Helen.

Millie slumped into a chair.

'I know I'm in a mess.'

'Who is to blame?'

Millie shrugged.

'Myself, I guess. I was so bored and lonely. Mum in hospital and Dad in prison. Aunt Alice does nothing but sit in the corner of the room and complain

. . . when you billeted that hooligan wi' me, I was attracted to him.'

'He's hardly good-looking, and you are pretty, Millie.'

'He flattered me, and I didn't suspect anything when he asked questions about the neighbours. Before I knew where I was, I'd become his accomplice.'

'Is this the first time you have been in trouble, Millie?'

'I've sailed close to it on a number of times,' she admitted.

'But, never as close as this?'

'Not wi' guns and knocking people out. Mind you, I've seen plenty of violence . . . the way Dad treats Mum.'

'You never did any of the hitting — Steve or the Commander?'

'Oh, no . . . but I was there.'

'Thank goodness, nobody has been badly hurt. You would have been in deep trouble.'

'What's likely to happen to me?'

'You acted bravely, just now — and it is obvious you have dropped Stott for good. That could count in your favour — if someone was willing to speak up for you.'

'But, the police will have to know?'

'Yes — the villagers will see to that. But, Millie — I'll speak up for you.'

Millie found a mellowness in her heart that she never knew existed. She couldn't remember anyone offering to really help her out of trouble before. They usually criticised and bullied so that she built up a temperament of resentment and stubbornness. Like the dislike she held for Steve Day for giving evidence that sent her father to prison, yet if she was strictly honest, she had to admit, her father got what he deserved, and she had no right to be hateful towards Steve.

'Will you really?'

'It is a promise — providing you speak the truth, all along the line.'

Millie nodded.

'The truth often comes hard. I'm too suspicious of people.'

Helen caught the girl admiring

Tommy's photograph, and it made her cross.

'That was cruel of you, tormenting me over Tommy.' Millie pouted.

'I admit I wasn't truthful all of the way.'

'How do you think I felt . . . worried stiff, trying to get news from Highport about Tommy's safety, then you suggest that he never left this side of the Channel to go to Paris,' Helen chided her.

Millie gave Helen a startled look.

'Oh, but Tommy was never in Paris Monday!'

'You still stick to that story? Why!'

'I was with Tommy on Monday night . . . and I happen to know he was in the district, all day. In fact I am certain he hasn't budged since.'

'Are you insisting that Tommy picked you up?'

Millie nodded, then hesitated and changed her mind.

'Not picked me up. I have met him several times before.'

'Where?'

'Here — in Haven Bay.'

'Right under my nose!'

'Tommy's visits were secret, usually when you were organising things with Steve Day.'

'This is scandalous!' protested Helen, horrified.

'I am telling the truth . . .'

'Tommy promised to meet me at Highport on Tuesday, when he returned from the continent. The fact that you say he never crossed the Channel, makes him out to be a cheat and a liar.'

'No, Miss — Tommy is a good man. Please don't call him a cheat.'

'The man I thought I was going to marry was good,' said Helen. 'Until you sowed these seeds of doubt in my mind.'

'Something really explosive happened on Monday,' recalled Millie. 'I am sure before it happened, Tommy was your man . . .'

Helen held her breath.

'Are you going to give me an

explanation?' she demanded.

'It wasn't a chance lift I got from Canterbury Hospital to Highport, and I didn't miss the last bus. Tommy brought me home, because he took me to Canterbury to see my Mum.'

Helen said, crossly:

'I am wondering if you are past helping, Millie.'

'Is that because I know Tommy?'

'It is sordid,' said Helen, wrinkling her nose.

'Why?'

'For heaven's sake, Millie. There have been times when I wondered if Tommy was too old a man for me. He's gone thirty — and, well I'm much younger.'

'He doesn't look anywhere near thirty.'

'He is thirty-five to be precise,' declared Helen.

Millie said, earnestly:

'If you think Tommy has been running about wi' me, then forget it. I am just fifteen, as everyone in the cottage found out, yesterday.'

'What about this trip to Canterbury?'

'He took me to see my mother in hospital.'

'Is that true?'

'There is an explanation why Tommy never went to Paris on Monday. Mum had to have an operation. She wanted to see me when it was all over.'

'Then, why didn't Tommy tell anyone. Even his parents thought he was on the ferry . . .'

'Can't you understand why?' murmured Millie.

'I am too confused to understand anything. Where does your mother come into this?'

'I suppose because she is Tommy's age.'

'What does that mean?'

'She was Tommy's first love, and I reckon, even when she married Dad, it never died.'

Helen felt bitter.

'I never knew the man,' she confessed.

'When Tommy heard that Mum had

been rushed to hospital, and was fighting for her life, then he raced to visit her. But, who could he tell?'

'He could have told me. I would have understood?'

'Would you, Miss . . . the name o' Clegg stinks for miles round here. Besides, there wasn't time. Tommy cancelled his business trip and hared off to the hospital. He hung around all day waiting for news, then in the evening when it was pretty sure that Mum had pulled through, Tommy came over to collect me.'

'Then he spent all day on Monday at the hospital.'

'Yes.'

'Well, I don't know,' whispered Helen.

'Is it hard to take, Miss?'

Helen shrugged.

'I must not be selfish. Your mother probably needed Tommy's comfort more than I ever did. But, you don't know how your mother is — not since the snowdrifts closed up this village.'

'There was no way of telling,' said Millie. 'But, if Tommy is with her, then I know she will be alright. I'm sure they are in love.'

'But, your mother isn't free . . . '

'A man who spends his time in and out of prison isn't the one to look after my Mum. I want her to be free. I want Tommy Carr to be one of the family. Maybe, we'll stand a chance of living then.'

Helen sank on to the bed and stared out of the window.

'Yes, Tommy is a good man. But, I wished I had got to know him better — more truthfully,' she concluded.

14

Helen was cold and hungry, and in the small back room, Jim West was coughing again.

Millie offered to go and see him, and Helen did not mind her going. She would have gladly been left alone for the rest of this day if it had been possible.

She felt humiliated because she had worn her grief for Tommy on her sleeve, and now, after Millie's startling disclosure it all appeared so phoney.

Millie had asked Helen not to blame Tommy. He was going through a rough patch because of his big heart, but Helen could not ignore the fact that Tommy was playing a double game. He was supposed to be in love with her, yet he was making secret visits to Haven Bay to see Millie's mother.

The secret visits hurt Helen, and she

could not wholly accept Millie's insistence, that they were just friendly visits to satisfy Tommy that his old love was coping while Clegg was in prison.

Millie had tried to make Helen understand that there was nothing in it. But, who would believe it. Tommy wanted to visit Millie's mother out of friendship. Everyone else would say he visited her because her husband was in prison. There was a sound reason why his visits were secret.

While Millie was giving comfort to Jim, Miss Pegler mounted the stairs, and announced:

'Stott wants to see you.'

Helen folded her arms and a stubborn expression invaded her eyes. For an instant she said nothing, but then remembered Steve's serious warning, that she must do as the thug ordered.

'What does he want?' she murmured.

The old nurse sniffed.

'He's mad . . . really mad!'

Helen glanced out of the window on to the sea front. The villagers had obviously been warned of the situation because they were assembling in the lea of the lifeboat station, and Steve was waiting to talk to them, acting as Stott's go-between.

'He has managed to turn our village upside down,' commented Helen.

Miss Pegler detected the young woman's lack of spirit.

'What is it, Helen — you look quite green?'

'I guess I have missed my breakfast.'

'No, it isn't that. You have gone without breakfast before. Is the strain too much?'

'I have just found out about Tommy Carr.'

Miss Pegler was puzzled. She knew Helen suffered anxiety on that first day when the news came through that the ferry had been sunk, but nothing positive had been learned since, simply because there was no way that information could reach the village.

'How on earth did you get any news about Tommy?'

'Millie told me . . . '

'Are we talking about the same Tommy — your Tommy?'

'Not my Tommy,' corrected Helen.

She regarded the old nurse, questioningly and asked softly:

'I expected to be the last one to know. How long has the village been gossiping about Tommy and Mrs. Clegg?'

'That was years ago,' protested Miss Pegler. 'Before Millie's mother got married.'

'No — it has started up again. Since Clegg has been in prison.'

'Has it! How on earth did they keep it a secret,' said Miss Pegler, indignantly.

Helen felt slightly less humiliated.

'You don't know about it?'

'No, Helen. And, you can rest assured that if I didn't . . . then nobody else in this village did.'

Helen clenched her teeth, and watched Steve move in among the locals. They stood hunched against the teeth of the savage weather, and Helen knew how desperately Steve wanted a break in the sky.

'I had better go and see what Stott wants,' she concluded.

'You shouldn't have to worry about Tommy Carr,' said Miss Pegler. 'That's the man for you — down there. He loves you, Helen. He wants to protect you. Look at the way he put himself between you and that thug's gun?'

'I rejected Steve for Tommy,' murmured Helen.

'We all make mistakes.'

'I can't face Steve . . .'

'Of course, you can!'

'I have made him feel second best,' admitted Helen.

'Steve is a patient man. Look at the way he's handling this situation. I am convinced he is waiting for the right opportunity to settle Stott's hash. Many people would have blown their top by now. I know I wanted to, just a while ago when Dr. Marsh called.'

'That was a delicate situation,'

reflected Helen. 'Dr. Marsh has a pistol. Steve had to avoid a gun battle.'

Miss Pegler sat on the bed, widened her eyes and said:

'Phew!'

Then as Helen walked to the door, she remarked:

'Lots of folk think Steve is too careful, but he gets there in the end. I reckon that's how it is going to be with you, Helen.'

Helen's mood was more relaxed when she went downstairs to face Stott.

He was nursing his gun, and his nerves were on edge. Helen suspected that he was sick, and the prospect of holding the whole village in the palm of his hand made him less reasonable than when she had first met him.

He said sullenly:

'We are going out in a moment, just to show the people I ain't fooling.'

'The villagers will listen to Steve. They have faith in him . . . '

Stott cut her short.

'I'm in charge of the village,' he

raged. 'Everyone does as I say.'

'Of course,' said Helen.

Stott wrested his eyes from the gun to study Helen at length. She was beautiful with proud features and bold eyes. A young woman well out of his reach, if he didn't have a thousand pounds in his pocket and a gun in his hands. He considered that nothing was out of his reach, now.

'You know you are coming to Highport wi' me?'

'As your hostage.'

'Don't be unkind, Helen.'

'What is going to happen when we land at Ostend?' Stott leered at her.

'Wouldn't you like to spend Christmas there wi' me. We can have loads of fun, an' I've got cash to burn.'

'My God — aren't you pathetic,' said Helen, with all the passion she could muster.

Stott's expression changed to one of hostility, and Helen found she could trust him that way far better than when he was trying to be pleasant.

'Maybe, you'll change your mind,' he growled.

'I am sure I won't.'

'Just don't make any slips. I'll be right behind you.'

'I won't forget.'

Stott climbed to his feet and prodded Helen with the gun. She swung away from him and trooped out of the cottage into the snow.

Despite Steve telling the assembly the facts of the situation, there were gasps of disbelief when they saw Stott holding Helen as hostage outside the cottage.

Many of the tough, rugged young men felt ashamed that this one hooligan could threaten lives the way he was doing. They wanted to do something violent and explosive, but Steve sensed their black moods and insisted on law and order. All the while he was in charge, they had to hold steady, and not run riot. He had explained that nobody would get hurt, providing Stott was given safe conduct across the bay, and he refused to risk a life for the sake of a young thug with a thousand pounds in his pocket.

Stott bawled to Steve above the biting wind.

'Take out your lifeboat crew — then everyone else go back indoors.'

Steve beckoned to his crew to step aside. Helen studied the sea of anxious faces that were left. The survivors, with hang-dog expressions on their faces, trying to convince themselves that this was none of their business, even if they had brought Stott ashore with them.

He never really was one of them. Just a hanger-on who joined in when there was a prospect of a lively night out.

Helen counted a number of people missing. She assumed that Dr. Marsh, after alerting the villagers and asking that word be passed on, had carried on with his medical visits. There was one sick survivor giving the doctor concern, while Jim West's condition was still rather topsy-turvy.

Commander Forbes wasn't among

the crowd, either. He was obviously suffering from the effects of being knocked out, and was resting.

Judd, the school caretaker was not there, and Helen could find no excuse for the old pensioner's absence.

Stott watched the locals begin to disperse, then in fanatical manner, he yelled:

'Anyone seen on the streets, and there will be trouble.'

Steve stood with his crew. They looked mutinously at the gunman, and then at the blue-faced, shivering Helen.

But, there was not one among them who was convinced that a gamble would be stimulating.

'We just can't give in — meek like, Steve,' said Joe Blackman, the lifeboat's bowman.

'Let's clear as much deck space as we can. We'll have supplies to bring back from Highport.'

'I'm not against risking the voyage to collect supplies for the village — but to get that lout to the headland, it's . . .'

complained Joe.

'It's common sense,' said Steve.

Stott waited until Steve and his crew went into the lifeboat shed, then he drove Helen back indoors.

During his absence, Miss Pegler had defied the gunman and prepared a meal for the hostages.

Millie had taken a tray up to Jim West, while the old nurse pushed a plate towards Helen.

Stott was livid with rage.

'Who said you could use up the rations?'

'You'll be on your way shortly — so what's it to you,' retorted Miss Pegler.

'You are driving me to ... ' threatened Stott, raising the gun.

Miss Pegler raised herself to her full height. She was still a handsome, well-kept woman and was scornful of the man who held the gun.

'If anything happened to me — or to any one of us,' she declared, 'this whole village would descend upon you like a pack of wolves . . . and if I've got to go,

I know I'd rather go clean and sudden.'

'Please, Miss Pegler — don't goad him!' cried Helen.

The old nurse smiled pleasantly at Helen, then glowered at Stott, with such a severe expression in her eyes, that the bullying gunman seemed compelled to listen to her.

'I'm taking good stock of your face, young man. I'll remember everything you have done to us peaceful folks in this village.'

Helen ushered her away before Stott went berserk.

'I wish you wouldn't, Miss Pegler. He may not be right in his head, and I mean that seriously.'

Miss Pegler mounted the stairs ahead of Helen. She paused at the top of the stairs, then before going along to her room to rest, she said, determinedly:

'That hooligan isn't going to get away with it. He has no idea the spirit there is in the village when the going gets rough.'

The old nurse stood poised by the

209

landing window, and she indicated the fiery Channel between the Straits.

'We had the German Army just twenty-odd miles away during the last war, throwing everything at us, and they didn't lick us . . . who does one thug with a shotgun think he is,' she concluded defiantly.

Helen went to her own room. She tuned in her transistor and the reception was bad. She listened for twenty minutes, and when a weather report promised that snow and high winds would hit the whole country for the fourth day in succession, she switched off in disgust.

Stott yelled at her to return downstairs. Helen went. He waved the gun in the direction of the kitchen.

'Make some tea.'

Helen did as she was bid, and served Stott with a mug of weak brew.

'What's this?' he protested.

'There isn't much tea in the caddie.'

Stott gulped at the tea and pulled a face.

'Tinned milk — hell, I'll be glad to get outa here. Champagne for me, tomorrow!'

The door crashed open, and the snowflakes whirled inside the front room.

Steve framed the doorway in his yellow oilskins and top boots. Binoculars were slung round his neck. He gave Stott a grim stare and announced:

'There is a small boat in trouble in the Channel. I'm taking out the lifeboat.'

He wasn't asking permission. Not even advising Stott. Simply making it plain that his job as a lifeboatman dominated everything else.

Stott narrowed his eyes.

'You ain't taking your boat any place, chum — not until I say so.'

'She's floundering on my patch,' said Steve.

'Let someone else go out to it.'

'Have sense, man! The snow is so thick nobody else will spot her. I only got a glimpse because the craft is in a direct line with the lifeboat station and not more than five hundred yards out.'

Stott grew suspicious.

'This is a trick. What fool would be out in a boat in this weather?'

'It isn't a trick.'

Stott ordered Steve to hand over the binoculars, then under threat from the gun, he was told to clear the lifeboat station. Then he went to see for himself.

15

Stott appeared to enjoy using Helen as his prime hostage. He held the gun close to her with one hand, while taking swift probes through the binoculars.

The snow that swept the sea front made it difficult to discern what was out there in the Channel, but finally, the gunman was satisfied that Steve had not tried to bluff him.

He tossed the binoculars to Steve.

'Yeah — it is a small boat.' He thought about it no more and added:

'Stop wasting my time.'

Steve went white with passion.

'You have seen for yourself!'

'Let 'em go under. 'Tis their own fault putting to sea.'

Their voices rang hollow in the large, tin-roofed shed that housed the lifeboat.

'That's murder!' Steve accused him.

'Fools have been lost at sea before,' argued Stott.

'I risked the necks of my crew rescuing you a few days ago,' Steve reminded him.

Then, totally ignoring the gunman, Steve turned his back on him, strode to the end of the lifeboat shed and began to shove open the large doors.

'Leave 'em!' screamed Stott.

Steve's crew ambled into view.

'Let's put to sea,' said Steve, calmly.

'I'll shoot Helen!' roared Stott.

Steve swung round. His crew were at his shoulders. They stared menacingly at Stott.

For a moment, there was deadlock. Helen, cold one minute in the freezing shed, started to perspire.

Stott's finger trembled on the trigger. Steve advanced.

'I'll tear you to pieces . . . '

Perhaps his threat was reminiscent of Miss Pegler's warning that the village would set upon him like a pack of wolves if any one of the hostages were harmed.

Steve was bluffing. He realised they outnumbered the gunman. They could rush Stott in the face of the gunshot. Some would get hurt badly, even killed. Stott might even carry out his threat and shoot Helen, before he was overpowered.

But, he relied on Stott still wanting to escape to the headland across the bay.

It was Stott that climbed down. He didn't lower his gun and instead issued Steve with an ultimatum.

'I will give you one hour to go out to that boat.'

'A deadline, eh!'

'That's right, chum.'

'I don't work to deadlines — not in this game.'

'If you ain't back within the hour, I really will start shooting,' concluded Stott.

'I am not coming back empty-handed,' promised Steve. 'But, I will be back. Make certain nobody gets hurt.'

Stott refused to wait and see the launching of the lifeboat, but the noise of the launching gear as the boat slid down the slipway groaned above the sound of the wind, and brought people on the sea front.

Defying his threats, Stott found himself ignored as the locals peered out to sea. It was tradition to wish their crew good luck and pray for the survivors.

The harsh weather soon drove the watchers back to their cottages, and although Helen was rudely prodded with the gun, she was convinced another crisis had blown over.

Stott drove Helen upstairs to her room. Millie was sitting in with Jim, while Miss Pegler had shut herself in her own room.

The thug sat by the door and commanded Helen to keep watch at the window.

'Tell me — when the lifeboat comes back.'

Helen automatically turned to her bedside table. Her hand was on the drawer, when Stott yelled at her.

'Hold it!'

Helen pursed her lips.

'I can see better through field-glasses. I have a pair.'

He still didn't trust her, and charged across the room, pulled open the drawer and inspected the contents.

'Alright — take the field-glasses,' he growled.

Helen kept watch. The flurries of snow caused a hard glare to her eyes as she scanned the sea smacking against the sea wall.

She found it not too difficult to pick out the lifeboat as it plunged forward seeking the floundering craft. The spray shot high into the air as the turbulent waves were thrust aside.

Then, she caught a glimpse of the small craft. It was a cabin cruiser, bucking like a wild horse as the waves attacked it, and making no progress, either forwards or astern.

Helen had seen enough of the Channel battles to realise that the small cabin cruiser could not stand such a buffeting for long, and she reflected that Stott was being generous when he fixed a deadline of one hour to effect the rescue. This little boat would not last the hour.

'What's happening?' demanded Stott.

'The lifeboat is getting closer — but it is a devil of a sea.'

'We'll know all about that, later on,' said Stott, with sinister relish.

'Steve's trying to get a line to the boat,' reported Helen. 'Safer than transferring the men ... but it is a highly-skilled operation.'

'I don't want a running commentary. Just tell me when they return.'

Stott's curtness silenced Helen, and for the next ten minutes she witnessed the lifeboat battling the sea to defend the small cabin cruiser.

She stared stonily out of the window as at first she lost sight of the lifeboat. Nothing happened for a while, except the day grew whiter and the visibility less.

Her heart stirred as the lifeboat

bucked into view. A massive wave held it aloft for a whole minute of torment before sucking it under as the wave fell.

The lifeboat vanished, bow to stern. Helen grew sick with fear, and the sea appeared suddenly empty.

Then the bold bows of the lifeboat emerged, shaking off the waves that clung tenaciously to her hull.

The lifeboat struck out for home, attacking the troublesome surf that squabbled for the right to dominate the shore.

Helen looked for the little boat in tow. The waves appeared too mighty, too grasping for it to have survived, then as Steve brought the lifeboat into the lea of the wall, Helen saw the cabin cruiser almost take off in the wash of the lifeboat's wake.

Lines were tossed inshore, and Helen watched eager hands secure the lifeboat to the bollards on the sea front. The crew were busy, bow and stern. The boat in tow snuggled up to her rescuer, and the two men aboard, concealed in massive waterproofs, were helped ashore.

Helen turned to Stott.

'They are home,' she announced.

'Wasted too much time,' he complained.

He signalled to Helen to lead the way downstairs. Steve came straight off the lifeboat and entered the cottage to tell Stott they would not be putting to sea again for another hour.

'Who is giving the orders?' demanded Stott.

'I am, where my crew is concerned. They need rest and a hot meal . . . so do I.'

Helen said:

'What about the men in the cabin cruiser?'

Steve flashed her a forbidding look as if he didn't want to discuss them.

'They are pretty exhausted, but a couple of the boys are looking after them.'

'What the hell were they doing out there?' growled Stott.

Steve wouldn't answer and Stott

grew suspicious. He didn't want any strangers nosing about the village, now that he had got control of the place.

'I want to talk to them,' insisted Stott.

'They are in no condition . . . '

'Fetch 'em!'

Steve hesitated, then before turning on his heel, he said, intently:

'I wonder if you would fire that gun?'

'You ain't going to take the risk to find out, are you?' sneered Stott.

The survivors were brought before Stott. Helen gasped in dismay at the sight of them. Stott grew white with anger, while Steve, hovered at the men's shoulders, still in the role of protector.

'You belong here!' screeched Stott.

Commander Forbes, patched up from his previous encounter with the thug, stared angrily through red and swollen eyes.

'We have met,' he croaked.

Stott rounded upon the tall, lean Mr. Judd from the school.

'I seen your face before.'

'That's right, me young cock. Not many folk forget Judd, the caretaker . . . and Judd, well he never forgets anyone.'

Behind them, Steve murmured:

'You two marvellous, old fools. Hearts of pure gold and guts of steel.'

'What do you mean by putting to sea and getting the lifeboat called out. I had booked the lifeboat . . . '

'So we heard,' Commander Forbes told him. 'We had to do something about that. Can't let you get away, y'know.'

'Got now't to lose at our age,' added Judd. 'We launched the boat from the Commander's davits in front of his cottage, and steered for the headland.'

'What did you reckon on achieving?' sneered Stott.

'If we had made the landing,' said Commander Forbes. 'We would have brought back a couple of policemen with guns — marksmen, mind you. It is the only way to deal with mad dogs.'

Stott laughed.

222

'Who are the mad dogs — launching a boat in that weather?'

'We felt we had a slender chance,' concluded Judd.

Both men looked ill and cold. Steve intervened and Stott made no move to stop him.

'Let's get you under cover and I'll arrange for Dr. Marsh to check you up.'

Stott gave the old men an evil glance as he dismissed them.

'If I miss that ferry — someone's going to pay for it.'

Helen said, observing the sullen sky, filled with snow:

'It is going to be a rough trip.'

'We are going.'

By noon, the Straits settled uneasily beneath a curtain of gloom. Black clouds rolled across the skyline, and a weird darkness invaded the coast.

The village, without power, and oil running short in the lamps was almost blacked out.

Stott sent Helen upstairs to get ready.

'Make it look as if you are going for a

trip across the continent. Wear something decent and carrying a shopping bag.'

Helen ignored him. She groped her way in the gloom to the bedroom. She intended selecting the heaviest clothing she possessed for the trip, and over them, she intended wearing her long duffel coat with the hood, despite its shabbiness.

Upstairs, Miss Pegler had borrowed the oil lamp from Helen's room. The one in Jim's room had gone out, and the old nurse had replaced it, when Jim's temperature had started to climb again.

Helen found a pencil torch with a dying battery and opened up her wardrobe.

She dressed in the impossible light, giving herself a bulky, well protected appearance by three layers of woollens.

She switched on the transistor. The battery on that was fading, too, but she managed to hear a lunchtime news bulletin followed by a weather report.

Helen's heart jumped for joy. Rain was spreading across the continent and should reach the Straits by evening.

She prayed that the rain would get here sooner. Anything to liberate the snowbound state of the village.

Miss Pegler crept in to wish Helen good-luck.

'Tell Steve — not to forget the oil. It will be deadly here without lamps.'

Helen and the old nurse embraced.

'It's like a nightmare,' whispered Helen.

'Be brave — put your faith in Steve.'

'And God!' murmured Helen.

Miss Pegler went along to her patient, and Millie came to see Helen.

There was barely enough light to see each other, but Helen could tell that the teenager was dreadfully nervous.

'What will happen to me when you have left, Miss Foster?'

Helen remained silent for a while. She had not thought of it.

'Miss Pegler will see that you come to no harm.'

'I was in with Stott from the start. The locals will not forget that.'

'That is true,' replied Helen.

'It seems strange, but all the while Stott is here, he gives me a sort of protection. But, after he's gone . . .'

'The locals are not a mob,' said Helen.

'Who knows what they will turn into. They have been made to suffer for several days and nights.'

'Millie — don't fret. There will be enough sensible people left to see that law and order is maintained.'

'Steve Day won't be here.'

'There are others . . . Dr. Marsh — ' Millie clung to Helen.

'Can you be sure about them. The doctor and the Commander are good friends. Look what happened to Commander Forbes . . .'

'Millie!' cried Helen. 'Let go — you are hurting me!'

16

Helen stirred on the bed. Her mouth was dry. Her arm ached, and she felt bitterly cold. She rubbed her arm and found it was bare. Little wonder she was cold. She had been left scantily clothed in the darkness, yet, she had a vague recollection of putting on three sweaters before Millie had entered the room.

She sat up. Her senses were numbed and when she tried to be more ambitious and get to her feet, she swayed dizzily.

Helen sank back on to the bed, and waited. She tried to put the pieces together.

Stott was holding her as his prime hostage. He had robbed the village postmaster of a thousand pounds, and while Haven Bay was completely snowbound, Stott had forced Steve

Day, the local lifeboat coxswain, to give him a safe conduct six miles across the bay to the headland town of Highport.

Helen was to make the trip, and then together with Stott, board the evening ferry that made the regular crossing to Ostend.

If, the hue and cry didn't go up, then it seemed unlikely that Helen would be harmed. But, if Stott's escape was thwarted, then he promised he would kill her.

What was going to happen when Stott and Helen got off the ferry at Ostend was anybody's guess.

Helen remembered being told to go and get ready for the trip. The room was in darkness, and in fact, because of a sudden darkening of the sky at noon, the village was almost blacked out.

Millie Clegg had come into the room, seized with fright, terrified as to what may happen to her when Stott quit the village.

Helen recalled the desperate way Millie had clung to her. Then she started to hurt her, squeezing and twisting her arm . . .

Helen touched the raw spot on her arm. The teenager was tough and strong, with a bully of a father. She had probably been forced to learn how to look after herself, and her lessons made her a formidable opponent.

Helen could only assume that she had dropped into a dead faint. She heard voices on the landing outside, and made her way across the bedroom to the door.

She recognised Miss Pegler's dry, matter of fact tone.

'It will be a week before the village returns to normal,' she declared.

'What a week,' replied the gruff voiced Dr. Marsh.

'If being cut off by snowdrifts wasn't enough . . . '

'This is only the third time I remember the village being cut off for more than three days. Three days is normal when the blizzards strike the Straits, but a week!'

'Soon after the war we were stranded for five days,' reflected Miss Pegler.

'Then there was the year when England had a hundred days of snow. In the fifties, and this village never saw the outside world for ten days.'

'But,' said Miss Pegler, gravely, 'we never had a gunman holding us to ransom.'

'No,' agreed the doctor. 'Fighting the elements is quite enough.'

'I wish the blighter hadn't got away.'

'The lifeboat will be over at the headland, shortly,' decided Dr. Marsh.

'That poor Helen Foster.'

'We can only wait.'

Miss Pegler's voice faded as she escorted the doctor to the top of the stairs.

'Thank you for the oil, Doctor. I'll be able to have a few lamps over the place, now.'

'Think nothing of it. Keep young Mr. West in his room for two more days, and I'll call again.'

Helen took a deep breath. The doctor

estimated that the lifeboat had almost arrived at Highport. How long had she been out cold?

She listened, and was aware that something was strange in the room. It was quieter. In fact, silent. The wind had dropped and the little cottage, no longer shuddered from the fierce battering of high tide against the sea wall.

She recrossed the room and stood against the cold window glass. For the first time in days, the snow had almost stopped, and in fact was giving way to a slanting sleet.

Helen went back to the door, tried it and found it locked on the outside.

She yelled from where she stood.

'Miss Pegler!'

Her voice attacked the darkness. The old nurse returned to the landing with Dr. Marsh behind her.

'Need some help, there,' Helen heard the doctor ask.

Miss Pegler leaned against the door.

'What is the matter?'

'The door has been locked . . . '

'Helen!' cried Miss Pegler.

'Yes . . . Millie locked me in.'

'Oh dear — I haven't a spare key.'

Helen's teeth began to chatter while she waited to be rescued, and she found her dressing gown hung behind the door. She climbed into it.

'Stand aside, Helen!' roared old Dr. Marsh.

He and Miss Pegler flew at the locked door, and they both tore into the room as the thin door gave way and swung off its hinges.

The doctor had left a powerful torch sitting on the floor outside. He now retrieved it and lit up the room.

'I thought you were on the lifeboat — held hostage,' murmured Miss Pegler, in disbelief.

'Millie changed places with me. She — twisted my arm until I fainted, then dressed in my sweaters and duffel coat . . . '

'I watched her leave — thinking it was you,' confessed Miss Pegler. 'It was so dark out there on the sea front, who could tell the difference. She wore the hood of the duffel coat up, and of course, nobody had anything to say to Stott, so he wouldn't suspect anything.'

'But, I wonder what happened when they got aboard the lifeboat,' mused Helen.

'They sat in the well of the boat. It was just as dark, there,' recalled Miss Pegler.

Dr. Marsh stroked his chin.

'Millie won't be found out until she gets ashore at Highport,' he assumed.

'Why has she done this?' asked Miss Pegler.

'She was terrified at being left behind in the village. Scared that the locals would turn on her,' said Helen.

Dr. Marsh patted the pocket that concealed his pistol.

'There will be no more violence in Haven Bay. I'll see to that.'

Miss Pegler sniffed.

'I'm thinking that maybe a leopard doesn't change his spots that quickly.'

'You think she came over to our side,

too readily?' suggested Helen.

Dr. Marsh was holding a surgery in ten minutes time.

'What's done is done . . . I must be on my way. Good afternoon, ladies.'

The doctor left Helen and Miss Pegler to discuss Millie's impulsive behaviour. The retired nurse was too concerned for Helen's chilled state to allow her to say another word until she had drunk a hot cup of coffee.

'It's only bottled stuff, Helen — with a little tinned milk. The corner shop is low in supplies until Steve gets back.'

'Anything, Miss Pegler. I'm dying of thirst.'

Miss Pegler lit a lamp in the kitchen, and made the coffee. They sat at the small table.

'I thought it was Millie in your room. She had stayed with Jim for a long while and I assumed she was resting. I must say, you gave me something of a turn, hearing your voice.'

'I had started to trust Millie,' admitted Helen.

'She's a Clegg . . . '

'She seemed sorry for what she had done.'

'I can't imagine her giving up her share of the loot. You can see what her little game is?'

'I am not sure,' said Helen.

'She's sticking with Stott. He dare not reject her, otherwise she'll give the game away.'

'Millie's blackmailing him into taking her with him?' queried Helen.

'She has got that kind of a vixen's brain,' concluded Miss Pegler.

Helen gnawed at her lip.

'Millie seemed so sincere.'

'About what?'

'The truth. I offered to help her.'

'You never know where you are with that sort of a girl,' reflected Miss Pegler.

'I don't know where I am,' admitted Helen.

'You mean — about Tommy Carr?'

Helen stared earnestly at the older woman.

'Could she have made all of it up?'

'She was speaking the truth when she told you that her mother and Tommy were young lovers more than twenty years ago.'

'But, what about now?'

'She could have spun you a yarn — about Tommy taking her to the hospital and sitting with Mrs. Clegg.'

'For what reason, Miss Pegler?'

'Millie won your confidence, didn't she?'

'That is true.'

'It is all she wanted to do.'

'Can a mere teenager be as cunning and tormenting as that?'

Miss Pegler smiled at the young schoolteacher.

'You know they can, Helen.'

Helen squeezed her hands together.

'What do I do about Tommy? I have made up my mind to dismiss him from my life completely. Now, I could be treating him unjustly, if I accept Millie's story as the truth.'

'Where was Tommy, last Monday — in Paris or sitting with Mrs. Clegg in

Canterbury Hospital. That is what you must find out, Helen.'

Helen blew out her cheeks.

'I didn't want to face Tommy again — now, it seems I will have to.'

Miss Pegler nodded wisely.

'We are not going to be snowbound for ever.'

Helen finished her coffee, then went back to her bedroom and got dressed.

She looked along the curve of the coastline at the well-lit towering headland, and her gaze followed the lights down to the harbour, then to the channel ferry at berth.

It was the first time for days, that the visibility had allowed the lights of Highport to be seen from the village, six miles away.

The sleet had turned to fine rain, and now that she was feeling perfectly recovered after her experience at Millie's rough hands, Helen decided to brave the wet darkness and go out to visit Commander Forbes and Jubb, the school caretaker, both of whom had suffered exhaustion in their brave attempt to cross the bay to fetch help.

Helen called upon the old Commander first. He should have been in bed, but a party of villagers had volunteered to return the battered cabin cruiser to the boat davits that were suspended on the paved forecourt outside the Commander's sea front cottage, and the old man stood at the window of his bedroom, bellowing Naval drill to the men as they clumsily hoisted the craft high and dry.

'Separate the falls!' roared Commander Forbes.

The boat handlers looked vaguely at each other. There was some confusion when the cabin cruiser started to slide stern first to the ground, and the Commander yelled in panic.

'Hoist, you fools!'

The craft remained suspended drunkenly between the davits, and while communications between the Commander and his boat crew suffered, Helen smiled at the comical scene and carried on to the caretaker's cottage, next to the school.

He was a no better patient than was the Commander, and explaining to Helen, that he had heard the noise of engines in the distance, he had climbed to the attic and kept a look-out through his powerful telescope.

'Come on up, Miss Foster,' welcomed Judd.

Helen tried to be indignant, and then climbed the wooden steps that gained access to the well-equipped loft.

Judd had thrown open the fanlight in the roof so that he could hear from what direction the noise was coming from, but he had to admit his hearing was far from keen, these days.

'I can't hear a thing,' said Helen.

'It comes and goes,' said Judd.

He swung the telescope and viewed the scene towards Foreland Hill.

'I thought maybe the snow ploughs were getting through but there 'aint now't up that way.'

He swung the telescope towards the

headland, and enjoyed the pleasure of seeing the well-lit harbour, full of boats and the bright, Cross-Channel ferry.

'Missed seein' what's been going on along the coast,' he admitted.

Helen gave a start.

'There is a noise!'

'Aye — you heard it?'

'Listen?'

Both held their breaths.

'It's from up there,' said Helen.

'You mean — aloft?'

'The sky!' insisted Helen.

Judd crouched low and tilted the telescope. He stared meticulously through the lense for three minutes solid, then shouted:

'Got 'im!'

Helen listened to the machine circling overhead. The first sign of life from the outside world since the blizzard more than four days ago.

'A helicopter,' declared Judd. 'And, I reckon she's looking for us!'

17

Helen looked down upon the village from her lofty perch, and realised what a difficult task the helicopter had in pin-pointing his target.

Except for a number of faintly glowing oil lamps that were placed at wide intervals over the village, Haven Bay was merely a splash of white along the uneven coastline.

Judd moved away from his telescope.

'The pilot can't hover up there for ever.'

'Is there any way we can show him in?'

Judd recalled his wartime experiences, and nodded:

'We must light flares on the ground.'

'There will be some in the lifeboat station.'

Judd began to descend from the loft, while Helen stole a second to scan the headland through the telescope. She lowered it, and Judd detected the disappointment in her expression when she joined up with him outside the cottage.

'Looking out for the lifeboat, were you, Miss?'

'I hoped I might catch a glimpse.'

Judd shook his head.

'Steve hasn't made it, yet.'

'If I could have spotted the lifeboat, it would have made me feel relaxed.'

'Nay, the waves are too high, and you wouldn't see the lifeboat's bow beam from that distance, especially as she's movin'.'

'Gives me the shivers to think what may happen,' confessed Helen.

Judd and the schoolteacher set off to tramp through the snow. They were in a hurry, knowing that the helicopter in the night sky would not search for ever.

Underfoot was treacherous. The snow was packed tight on top, and frozen solid beneath. The rain that fell, froze when it reached the ground. The wind, while lacking the gusto of the past few days of blizzard, got through to the bones.

On the sea front, Judd remarked that the Channel was still too full for calm sailing as the waves licked hungrily at the sky.

Judd led the way into the lifeboat shed. Steve's office was still in a shambles from the gunman's attack, but the old man, who had served as a lifeboatman for many years before drawing his pension, remembered where everything was stored.

'Let's warn the helicopter we know he's up there,' decided Judd.

He opened a cupboard and handed Helen a large rocket, then grabbed a box of flares.

Helen fixed the rocket into the stand outside the station, and Judd applied a match to it.

The rocket exploded and tore through the darkness, leaving a flare path in its wake.

The explosion so familiar on stormy

nights brought the villagers on to the sea front. Judd made use of everyone. They set out the flares on the ground, shared out the matches and lit the flares simultaneously.

The words 'Haven Bay' flared up towards the dark sky, and reminded Helen of some frivolous firework display, but nobody was laughing, as heads jerked upwards, hoping to catch a glimpse of the helicopter.

The noise of the engine droned closer, and the machine circled, then clawed its way across the village, hovering above the flare path.

The villagers moved back in the lea of their cottages as the machine descended.

The propellors roared and the snow swirled. The flares quietly died. The helicopter settled on the surface. The pilot climbed out and peered at the sea of faces who regarded him with more suspicion than welcome.

Helen walked forward with Judd, while upon hearing the maroon go up,

Commander Forbes had led his party of boat handlers along the sea front to see what the emergency was all about.

'Devil of a job finding you,' said the pilot.

'Good to see you,' said Helen, with a smile.

The pilot stared mysteriously at the blacked out village and the enormous piles of snow that hemmed in the cottages. He hunched his shoulders as the spray from the high tide spat at him.

'Brought you a radio set,' he announced.

Helen grew excited. Had Steve already reached Highport and reported the impossibility of communicating with the headland town?

'How did you know ours was busted?' asked Judd.

'I don't know anything. I'm just the delivery boy.'

'But, someone . . . ' suggested Helen.

'Sure, I got a message from the coastguard at Highport that he had lost contact with you.'

'You ain't from Highport?' queried Judd.

'No — from Manston. I don't suppose Highport had got a spare set, and they haven't got a helicopter to deliver it.'

'The coastguard must have guessed our radio had broken down,' mused Helen.

The pilot asked for a hand to unload the gear, and when he was helped with the radio set into the lifeboat shed, he gave a surprised whistle at the damage.

'Broken down! What happened?'

'A thug ran amok,' reported Helen.

'I've been held up by the weather,' said the pilot, apologetically. 'Looks as if you people needed help here.'

Commander Forbes pushed his way forward. He was the man who knew most about working the radio when Steve was away, and the sudden arrival of outside help gave him an idea.

He introduced himself and got the pilot's name.

'Look, here — Gibson. We want to nab that blighter Stott. How soon can we get this radio link set up?'

Gibson wanted to help, although his services were needed elsewhere. His machine had been grounded all the while the blizzards had raged along the coast.

He rubbed his jaw at the sight of the broken wires and attachments where Stott had destroyed the original set.

'Might take a couple of hours to fix up.'

He glanced towards his machine and added:

'But, I could try and locate Highport over my own radio.'

Gibson made no promises. His own radio was short range and weather conditions were still not good for fair reception.

He got a good idea what the trouble was all about from Helen and then tuned his radio. After a lot of crackling and buzzing, Gibson laid the headphones aside and shook his head.

'Sounds like the whole population of the country is butting in on the same wavelength. Sorry for wasting time.'

He jumped down from his machine, and helped Commander Forbes rig up the replacement set in the lifeboat station.

Meanwhile, Judd had gone back to his look-out in the loft of his cottage and scanned the headland approaches for any sign of the lifeboat. He spent an hour watching, and when he returned he had to make the grim announcement, that he hadn't been able to locate the lifeboat.

'Steve hasn't docked her, that's for sure — 'cause I can see all the boats lying still in the 'arbour.'

'Is the ferry . . . ?'

Judd pointed in the direction of the headland. Visibility was improving as the night wore on.

'You can see the ferry from here — all lit up from bow to stern.'

'Then — why can't we see the lifeboat?' demanded Helen, hotly.

'The sea is choppy outside the harbour. It takes skill to get a lifeboat through the outer wall,' replied Judd.

Gibson swept a load of unwanted wires on to the floor, and turned to the Commander.

'Try that!'

Commander Forbes knew the frequencies of both the coastguard station at Highport and the radio aboard the lifeboat.

He started to turn the knobs and stared at the wavelength pointer travelling round the dial.

Helen peered over his shoulder.

'What's happening?' she whispered.

Commander Forbes shook his head. A lot of advice was thrown in from radio enthusiasts in the crowd cluttering up the doorway of the station.

Gibson regarded the luminous dial of his watch. He'd got to return to base, pick up a load of fodder and make a drop along the snowbound Downs, where a cluster of small farms had sheep trapped by the drifts.

He caught Helen's eye. She faced him.

'I am sorry, Miss. I shall have to leave you to it. The radio is working fine, but you'll just have to be patient and keep trying.'

'Thank you, Mr. Gibson. Let's hope we are not too late.'

Gibson glanced at the gloomy village.

'You have got a bad situation here. If I can get back, in the morning — what do you need most?'

'An engineer to get the power back, I suppose. It is dreadful without lights and telephones.'

'What about supplies?'

'We are praying that Steve will bring them back from Highport by boat.'

'Of course . . . but you will have got in touch with Highport before then,' Gibson assured her.

He climbed into the helicopter and made a straight ascent, billowing the snow along the sea front.

Helen went back to the station. Commander Forbes gave her a rueful look.

'I have given up trying to contact Steve — I have switched to the coastguard at Highport.'

'Please, Commander . . . '

'Helen, my dear. Stott will have ordered radio silence for the crossing. I am convinced of that. He's not taking any chances of Steve giving any advance warning.'

The retired Naval man returned to full concentration on the radio set, trying to link up with the coastguard at Highport.

Everyone waited tensely. Ten minutes later, the Commander's voice was answered.

He swivelled in his chair and boomed at the crowd:

'We are through!'

It was such a vital moment, that a cheer went up, but the Commander's stern message to Highport, soon quelled that.

'A thug named Stott — armed, and his accomplice, Millie Clegg, wanted for robbing the village post office and two other incidents of assault. Is forcing Steve Day to give him safe conduct to the headland, where Stott plans to board the ferry. Stott is dangerous and armed. I repeat — dangerous . . . over!'

Confirmation of the message came back, and with it, information that floating wreckage at the entrance to the outer harbour wall was preventing boats entering the inner harbour. The lifeboat was held up.

Commander Forbes rested the earphones, and called for volunteers to stay on duty by the radio throughout the night. Helen was among the volunteers, and the Commander drew up a rota, each volunteer doing a four-hour watch round the clock. He then briefed the volunteers how to operate the radio, and finally worn out after such an eventful day, he crept home to bed.

Helen took over the first watch. The crowd dispersed and left her alone.

She made herself a mug of coffee from Steve's food store, and spent a while tidying up his quarters.

The high pitched 'beep-beep' from the radio took her to the set instantly. She listened in. It was the coastguard from Highport. Cheerful and chatty. The weather forecast for tomorrow was cold and dry. Snow ploughs would be out in force all along the coastal roads. With luck, Haven Bay would be relieved by late afternoon. Before the coastguard ended his call, Helen asked, desperately:

'What's the news about, Steve?'

'The tide is clearing away the wreckage — but slowly.'

'How long before he reaches harbour?'

'Another hour, maybe.'

'That long?'

'The ferry is due out . . . he'll have to give way for that.'

'I see,' murmured Helen.

'That isn't bad news, is it? This thug Stott — he'll miss the ferry,' concluded the coastguard.

'That's just it. He could go berserk.'

'I wouldn't worry, Miss ... as a matter of fact, I can see three cars of policemen along the quay from where I am standing.'

Helen closed down the set. She spent another nervous hour, waiting for more messages. None came. She turned and looked towards the headland. The lights were far less over the town now, than they were an hour ago.

Then she saw a blurr of light, and realised it was the ferry leaving the waterfront.

Helen watched the ship's progress, and started to imagine Stott's mood when he realised his plan had been shattered by something that had been impossible to take into consideration.

She found a pair of binoculars and held them to her eyes. The ferry slipped quietly out of harbour and then braced herself for the rough Channel crossing.

The sea was high, but the snow had faded. Visibility was now more than fair.

Helen grew increasingly nervous

concerning the situation on Steve's lifeboat.

She sat in front of the radio set, twirled a knob and got on the same wavelength as Steve's radio.

There was just a chance now, that he had broken radio silence. The line was dead for a full minute, then an ear splitting crack. A voice invaded the line. Urgent and desperate.

'Lifeboat to shore . . . '

Helen overheard the coastguard at Highport accept the message.

'Shore to lifeboat . . . come in?'

The voice from the lifeboat:

'Please call ambulance. There has been a shooting aboard.'

Helen withdrew her breath as if she had been struck. The voice had not belonged to Steve. Yet, he always relayed the messages.

18

Helen's first reaction was to contact the coastguard at Highport, but she could see through her binoculars, that the lifeboat's bows were now nudging through the sheltered waters of the harbour.

There would be too much activity on the quayside when the boat berthed before any precise details as to what had happened during the arduous crossing could be assembled.

The lifeboat appeared tiny to Helen, and the binoculars were not powerful enough to pick out any figures on the craft.

She observed the boat's progress into harbour, then it was lost amid the haze and lights of the waterfront. Helen lowered the binoculars and made herself wait.

She tapped the table with her fingers,

a nervous habit that was strange to her. She quickly learned what tension was all about. There had been times, when she concluded she would never be able to stand the strain of waiting for Steve, when he took the lifeboat out on a mission.

But, the fear she experienced, while she waited for news after hearing that dramatic message, she was convinced could never be equalled.

If she survived the next hour without losing control, Helen was sure she could be the wife of a lifeboatman without having to fear a more pro-longed trial.

The coastguard was aware of Helen's deep concern, and she thought it indifferent of him not to relay a message across to her, confirming that Steve was unharmed.

Her watch was almost up, and still she had heard no word. Throwing caution to the winds, she tuned in on the Highport frequency.

It was several more minutes before

the hearty voice of the coastguard replied to her.

'Can you tell me anything about the Haven Bay lifeboat, please?'

'Very little, lass. A lot of excitement down there on the quay.'

'I picked up the lifeboat's message to you. It said there had been a shooting aboard!'

'That's right. I telephoned for an ambulance.'

'Who got hurt?'

'I can't say, lass . . . I can't leave my post, and my only contact with the harbour is by telephone, and since the lifeboat docked, the harbour master's phone has been jammed with calls.'

'Is there a chance that you can find out and let me know?'

'I'll do my best.'

Helen reluctantly closed down the set, and did some more waiting. Then just before she was due off duty, the coastguard got in touch.

'Not much new, lass. The police have arrested a man, but everyone off the lifeboat are making statements to the police.'

'I see — will you keeping trying. I'm terribly anxious . . . '

'Aye, I can detect that,' concluded the coastguard.

A volunteer came to relieve Helen. He was the owner of the corner shop, and known by everyone in the village as Peter.

'Get yourself to bed, Helen,' he said, waiting for her to vacate her chair.

He put her paleness down to living through a tense day, but when she protested in an agitated voice that she wanted to stay on duty, Peter knew there was something else.

'What is it?'

'There has been a shooting aboard the lifeboat . . . '

'That maniac!' seethed Peter. 'He promised nobody would get hurt. What happened, Helen?'

'I can't find out. The lifeboat was delayed entering harbour because of wreckage blocking the outer wall, and I know for sure that the ferry sailed — without Stott.'

Peter nodded solemnly.

'That character was crazy enough to seek revenge.'

'It crossed my mind, that perhaps he blamed Steve for not keeping his side of the bargain.'

'You must not think that way,' advised Peter.

'Steve always relays the messages from the lifeboat. He's in charge. The message I overheard wasn't Steve's voice.'

'Helen — you can't be positive about that. Voices over the radio are distorted.'

Helen shook her head, stubbornly.

'Once, I picked up Steve's voice over my transistor. There was no mistaking it.'

Peter grunted.

'Well, try not to worry and go and catch up on some rest.'

'But, if a message comes through?'

'I'll come and give you a call.'

Helen shifted away from the radio set.

'Thank you, Peter.'

She left the lifeboat station and returned to her cottage. A fire glowed in the grate, and Miss Pegler sat hunched over it in the gloom.

'Why aren't you in bed?' asked Helen.

'Couldn't sleep.'

'You have had a strenuous few days. You ought to be resting.'

Miss Pegler smiled.

'I suppose I am too curious to know how it all turned out. Millie changing places with you, and the treacherous crossing. The excitement kept me awake.'

'The lifeboat has reached Highport — just,' said Helen, sitting on the rug in front of the fire and warming her hands.

'Phew — all this time to cover six miles. It must have been an awful voyage. Thank goodness, they got there safely.'

Helen turned her head sharply.

'I don't know about that. There was a shooting aboard.'

'Oh, God — no!'

'Been trying to discover what happened. But, the situation is very confused over at Highport.'

'We should have jumped on Stott, while he was here,' said Miss Pegler, grimly.

'Police are taking statements,' reported Helen.

'I imagine they want the whole story from start to finish,' murmured Miss Pegler.

'It began with a boatload of survivors from the ferry,' mused Helen. 'Look, how it has ended.'

'I know. Makes you wonder if Haven Bay will ever be the same.'

'Peter has promised to give me a call if there is further news,' disclosed Helen.

'We both don't have to stay awake — and I'm not sleepy,' said Miss Pegler.

'I couldn't sleep,' insisted Helen.

But, after sitting together in silence for a while, both women dozed by the fire, and when a violent knocking vibrated through the cottage, Helen opened her eyes with a start, and thought that another gale had blown up.

It was a few seconds, before she became conscious of the situation, and was angry at her lapse.

She hurried to the door. Peter stood there, shivering in the awful cold.

'Something is coming through, Helen.'

Helen, coatless, skated across to the lifeboat station. She fell in front of the radio set and took the message that was being relayed. The first words made her catch her breath in utter relief.

'Steve . . . it is you. Thank God!'

'I had to hear your voice,' replied Steve. 'Just to make sure.'

'What happened, Steve — I know about the shooting . . .'

'That story will keep.'

'But, Steve!'

'Sorry, love. I can only have a few

seconds on this line. The shipping is starting to move in the Channel and we have to keep the lines of communication here open.'

'If you only knew how I have suffered,' protested Helen.

'Because — you love me?'

'Of course!'

'Love — as soon as the tide turns we'll be on our way home.'

'Then, hurry . . . I can't wait.'

'Tell the village we are loading the lifeboat with supplies, and we are picking up mail and newspapers, fresh food and milk. We'll have a Ball, when we dock.'

'I'll tell the village.'

'Helen — just one thing more. What about Tommy Carr?'

Helen found herself covered with embarrassment.

'I had forgotten about him.'

'Do you want me to find out anything?'

'Why should you?'

'Peace of mind for both of us. A

couple of telephone calls might settle things.'

Helen said, tersely:

'I think it is up to Tommy to get in touch with me. The roads will be clear tomorrow.'

Steve sounded satisfied and he concluded:

'I think Millie told you the truth — and thank God, you are safe!'

The line went dead. Helen was struck with a cold feeling concerning Steve's final remark.

Why was he so convinced that Millie was a truthful girl? Had they been wrong about the girl's motives in swopping places to enable her to stick close to Stott.

Helen felt uneasy for the rest of the night, although Miss Pegler assured her, that now Steve was safe and well, she could go to bed.

Helen went up to her room. Her movements on the stairs must have disturbed Jim. He started coughing, twisting in his bed and Helen heard him knock a bottle flying in the darkness.

Helen went along to him, throwing a faint light from her pencil torch ahead of her.

'What's happened?' groaned Jim, sleepily.

'Nothing serious. You sent your medicine flying.'

Helen picked up the bottle.

'All intact . . . I had better give you some, now I'm here.'

Helen helped him with his cough medicine. She heard Jim swallow it, clear his throat and then say:

'Something is different?'

'Yes, Jim.'

'I have slept for a long while, I guess.'

'Stott and Millie left.'

'I see — any news?'

'The lifeboat reached Highport.'

Helen did not worry the sick man with further details, but instead tried to cheer him up by telling him that with the improved weather allowing snow ploughs to be out in force at dawn, the village would soon be back to normal.

'Normal,' grunted Jim.

Helen suspected that his unhappiness and stress was delaying his recovery. She knew that Jim could not hope for a return to normal. He'd got to pick up the pieces and start afresh.

'You will be able to leave Haven Bay.'

'For what — four blank walls of an empty flat?'

'Jim — these things happen.'

'I know. I'm not the only guy to lose his pretty wife to her dynamic young boss. It happens.'

'When you are fit, Jim, you will be able to face it.'

'Helen — you sound very content.'

She stepped back from the bedside.

'I feel lucky,' she admitted, and retired to her room.

Daybreak emerged, dry and cold. The sea front became a busy place as under a clear sky, the villagers attacked the deep lying snow and tossed shovelfuls of it over the sea wall, where it landed on the shingle at low tide.

It had been the safest low tide for a week, with the surf hardly reaching the foot of the wall.

Before noon, a grey sky turned to faint blue, and a weak sun broke through.

Sunlight on the snow looked a pretty sight, and although the corner shop was dishing out the last of the dwindling supplies, the villagers chatted cheerfully as they queued.

Helen did her share of snow shifting, and then walked along the sea front, feeling the pleasant warmth of the sun on her face.

Across the Channel, the sun glinted on the cliffs of France. Helen listened to the tide begin to lap against the wall, so gently and delicately as if to respect the silence following the hostile weather.

She stood there, watching the tide turn, and then wandered along to the school.

She found Judd, lighting fires in the school to keep the place aired, and asked if she might go up to his loft and scan the countryside through his telescope.

'Help yourself,' agreed the caretaker.

Helen got her sights on the coastal road, where the snow ploughs were sending up dense clouds of snow, then she swivelled round the coastline, until she located the headland.

The tide looked very full in the harbour, and when after a couple of minutes wait, she spotted the lifeboat easing her way clear of the harbour, her heart gave a joyful leap.

She darted down the flight of steps and told Judd that Steve was on his way home.

During the morning, the ones with more knowledge of tides and currents than Helen possessed, calculated how long it would take Steve to make the crossing.

If the fair weather prevailed, the lifeboat would be home and dry within the hour.

Before the lifeboat arrived, however, Gibson the helicopter pilot flew in with a couple of engineers and a mass of repair equipment to see if lights and telephones could be restored.

Gibson took off again to continue his missions all along the coast and Downs.

The engineers tackled the problem of getting a blown-out transformer working, while moving sweetly across the bay towards Haven Bay, Steve was bringing home the lifeboat.

The villagers scuttled through the melting snow to line the sea wall and welcome the crew. Helen fought for a place in the front.

Steve was at the wheel. Ashen-faced, his head swathed with bandages.

19

The lifeboat's homecoming was not a scene of great emotion. The tolerant people of Haven Bay had seen it so many times during the course of a normal year. The sight of an injured Steve did inspire questions to be asked, and together with a curiosity of wanting to know what had happened to the young thug and his teenage moll, quite a noisy hub-bub was created along the sea wall.

Joe Blackman, the lifeboat's burly and veteran bowman took charge of the docking and when the boat was secure at the foot of the slipway, Steve killed the motors, looked ashore and raised his hand at Helen.

He left the unloading of the supplies and the housing of the lifeboat to his crew and the villagers, then climbed the slipway to the top of the wall.

'Hello, love.' he grinned.

Helen walked into his embrace. She wanted to take him out of sight of all these people and stay with him alone, but the elderly Dr. Marsh shouldered his way forward, gave a discreet cough and said:

'Who patched you up, Steve?'

'First aid chap at Highport.'

'Had a check up?'

'There was hardly time.'

'Come over to the surgery.'

'I have only a headache, Doc!'

'Don't argue with me, lad,' said the doctor.

Steve pulled a face at Helen and squeezed her hand. He promised to see her after the doctor was finished with him.

Helen decided it was too exciting a day to return indoors, besides the whole village was working shoulder to shoulder to get the place back to normal.

A chain had been formed to unload the supplies. Helen saw cartons of fresh milk, crates of fruit, baskets of new bread and sides of bacon and meat being brought ashore.

The family who ran the corner shop, with the help of some young men with shovels had cleared a track to bring a van on to the sea front, and the van was being quickly loaded and despatched to the shop.

Mr. Peters from the Post Office had claimed two sacks of mail, but before he could move off to start sorting the letters, a constable and a detective shipped over from Highport were asking him questions, obviously about the robbery.

As the lifeboat's decks grew bare once more, Helen caught Joe Blackman's eye.

He gave her an encouraging smile and Helen ventured forward.

'Quite a night,' he remarked ruefully.

'Yes,' she murmured.

'Steve is a tough nut. He isn't badly hurt.'

'Will you tell me what happened, Joe?'

The lifeboatman hesitated.

'Should I?'

'I have a feeling, Steve won't tell me.'

Joe stepped ashore and sat on a bollard. He rubbed dry salt from the back of his hands.

'I guess he'd find it difficult. Never the one to shout the odds about himself.'

'How did he get hurt?'

'I guess — it was because he was protecting you.'

'I was here — at Haven Bay!'

'Sounds like a puzzle, don't it?'

'I think I know what you mean, Joe.'

He grunted. The crossing was rough and slow. They hit bad currents, and Highport was never an easy place to enter when the sea was angry. The entrance to the outer harbour was blocked with wreckage from the sunken ferry, and Steve had anchored the lifeboat until a more favourable tide swept the wreckage away.

'By then, it was obvious our passenger wasn't going to be in time to board the outgoing ferry.'

'I can imagine his mood,' murmured Helen. 'His plan to escape was an obsession.'

'Aye — he went proper nuts! Screaming at Steve to take the boat through the wreckage.'

'And, brandishing his gun, I suppose?'

'Aye — a real fanatic! Steve couldn't take the boat through. He could have lost his crew and his boat. His job and reputation. It was too much to expect.'

'Something that Stott would never understand,' mused Helen.

'It grew ugly from then on. Stott threatened to shoot Steve — but he never got the chance.'

Joe licked his salty lips and disclosed that the girl in the duffel coat, they all thought was Helen, suddenly climbed to her feet and hurled herself at the gunman.

Stott, without scruples had shot her.

'Millie!' cried Helen, in a choking voice.

'Nobody knew it was the Clegg girl . . . '

'She forced me to stay here, while she went with Stott. How badly . . . ?'

'Took the shot in the shoulder. She was in a bad way by the time we got to Highport.'

Helen hung her head.

'That might — it ought to have been me.'

'Don't blame yourself. In fact, Steve thought it was you. My God — in all my life I have never seen a man in such a rage. He simply waded into Stott. I'm sure it was Steve, who was the crazy one in that instant. We had to pull him off to save Stott's skin, and it was some time before Steve calmed down.'

'Steve could have been killed!'

'He took a blow from the butt of the gun across the temple.'

Helen gnawed at her lip and confessed to Joe:

'I am convinced Steve would never have told me.'

'I reckon he would find it difficult to

explain just how he feels about you, but we saw it. He'd walk straight into death for you, would Steve. Best get spliced wi' him, Helen. 'Aint another like him for miles.'

Joe moved off the bollard and supervised the housing of the lifeboat, and Steve called Helen as he emerged cheerfully from the doctor's surgery.

'Nothing to worry about,' he said, putting an arm round Helen.

'You should have gone to Highport hospital and had a check up.'

'Honestly — there wasn't time.'

'Because, you were concerned over Millie Clegg?'

Steve stopped in his tracks.

'How did you know, Helen?'

'If Millie saved your life, I know jolly well, you wouldn't have allowed her to go to hospital alone.'

'I had to,' admitted Steve.

'Will she pull through?'

'She lost blood . . . but when I left the hospital, the report was satisfactory.'

They stood together on the sea front enjoying the sun on a winter's day.

'You told me over the radio, Steve — that you were sure Millie was a truthful girl.'

'Yes — she was often misjudged.'

'I made up my mind she changed places with me, so that she would not let Stott out of her sight. She wanted her share of the loot, and what had happened in the cottage earlier, was just an act.'

'Millie told me why she changed places with you, Helen.'

'Why, Steve?'

'Before they whipped her along to the operating theatre, she said, she was of no value to anyone. Not to Stott — not to the village. It made her useless as a hostage, and as soon as we docked she was going to blow it as far as Stott was concerned.'

'It never quite worked out,' said Helen.

'No.'

'If you had known it was Millie

aboard with Stott — would you have defied his gun, like you did, Steve?'

Steve leaned on the railings that bordered the sea wall and stared at the coast of France.

'I hope so. I hope I would have behaved exactly as I did. But, I can't really say.'

'Joe said you saw red — because you thought it was me that Stott had tried to kill.'

'Joe shouldn't have said that.'

'If he hadn't — I wonder if I ever would have known how you feel about me?'

'Let's find somewhere to sit down, and I'll tell you,' said Steve.

20

In the morning, the sunlight glimmered on the sea, and the gutters along the sea front gurgled as they swallowed the water from the thaw.

Helen had awoken to the unfamiliar clatter of the letter box, and donning her dressing gown she went downstairs and collected a bundle of mail.

She moved habitually about in the gloom for a few minutes, and then remembered that the engineers had restored the power, late yesterday evening.

She touched a switch and the room was flooded with light. She examined the letters. Mostly the initial delivery of Christmas cards. All but two of them for Miss Pegler. A neatly written envelope for herself and another letter for the retired nurse.

Helen put the kettle on the gas to

make the early morning cup of tea, and then opened her letter.

The date at the top showed the letter was written on the same day as the sinking of the ferry. A day to remember. The blizzards. The call out of the lifeboat. Her own desperate attempt to get over to Highport to meet Tommy Carr.

Helen read the letter with little patience. She could not blame Tommy for the letter being delayed, but she blamed him for not making up his mind.

The letter was brief and jerky, and the writer was obviously unsure how best to put his feelings on paper. He had meant to tell Helen, meant to tell her . . . he had repeated himself, before managing to confess that his love for Mrs. Clegg, despite her husband, was too strong for him ever to be really loyal to another girl.

Helen read no more. She understood that Tommy had problems, and she supposed if it could be worked, and

Mrs. Clegg and Millie could break away from the rogue of a man, who was neither husband or father, only in title, then Tommy would win her respect.

The only thing the letter did prove to her, was that Millie had been telling the truth.

Helen decided she must help the girl all she could, despite what the village thought about the teenager.

Helen made a pot of tea and took cups to Miss Pegler, luxuriating in the warmth of the sunshine invading her bedroom, and Jim West, brooding over his future.

She returned downstairs, drank a cup of tea, then dressing casually and colourfully, she went for a brisk walk along the sea front.

Traffic was managing to get through on the single track that the snow ploughs had furrowed out by working nonstop all night.

The regular village constable was patrolling a beat, and he bade Helen a solemn good-morning, although he was still smarting from the leg-pulls dished out to him by the young men in the village, who accused him of getting stuck in the snow on Foreland Hill, at a time when he was most needed inside the village.

The corner shop was putting on an inviting display of fresh goods, while in the High Street, the lights were on in shop windows, giving sparkling advertising to Christmas goods.

Helen made her way along to the school and saw Judd. She thought it would be appreciated if the village threw a party for the lifeboat crew, and together they agreed to enlist the help of the local ladies to organise it.

She peeped in at the lifeboat station on her way back to breakfast. Steve was tidying up his quarters, and Helen stayed to give him a hand.

He looked at her in a fascinating manner after all that they had said to each other the night previously.

'Where will we live, then?'

'In Haven Bay, Steve.'

'You are sure?'

'I am not going to quit this village,' insisted Helen.

'Then, I'll look for a cottage. We'll put down roots,' decided Steve.

'Yes, Steve. I feel I belong here.'

They embraced, and would have gone on embracing if footsteps hadn't disturbed them.

The detective and the constable brought over from Highport were seeking Helen to give them a statement concerning the Stott affair.

She told them about the boatload of survivors brought ashore from the lost ferry, and the one very bad apple among them.

After the detective had written down Helen's statement, he remarked:

'I guess that's the trouble with survivors. You can't select them, can you?'

Steve smiled.

'They are all the same to me. Helpless wretches, and you have to pluck 'em out of the sea, no matter who they are.'

'This'n caused you all a lot of bother,' reflected the detective.

'He did that,' agreed Steve.

The detective studied his notes.

'Now, I have to take a statement from Commander Forbes. Where does he live?'

Helen pointed to the cottage at the end of the sea front, where the cabin cruiser was suspended in lopsided fashion from the davits on the cottage's forecourt.

'That is the Commander's place,' she directed.

The policemen went on their way. Helen left, as well, passing young Dr. Marsh, who had just got back to the village after being stranded outside since the night of the blizzard.

His first patient was to be his own father, who after the elderly doctor's marathon efforts all the while the village was snowbound, had now gone down with a stiff dose of flu.

'Good morning, Miss Foster,' said Dr. Marsh.

'Good morning,' replied Helen, happily.

In the afternoon, as the snow ploughs made a greater impact upon the snowdrifts, traffic flowed almost unhindered.

The village bus en route to Highport stopped and picked up passengers. Two policemen from Highport boarded it, then later on, a specially chartered coach drew into the village and the survivors trooped onto it, taking them first to Highport and then dispersing them to their homes.

To Helen, it seemed like the end of an era in her life, but perhaps not so conclusive as the visit from the smartly dressed young woman, who stepped out of the taxi on to a sea front shimmering from the sunlight.

She approached Helen, an unfolded newspaper in her hand.

'Excuse me — this is Haven Bay?'

'Yes.'

'The village where some of the survivors from the ferry were landed?'

'We had some,' said Helen, quietly.

'Have they all left?' asked the young woman, dismayed.

Helen made a rapid calculation. Stott was in prison. One of the others was still too sick to move. The bulk of them had just gone by coach to Highport. That left — Jim West.

'Who are you looking for?' asked Helen.

'My husband . . . '

She stabbed at a list of names on the front page of the newspaper she held, and added:

'It says — Jim was saved and brought to Haven Bay.'

Helen confirmed it was true. The attractive young visitor went on talking as if she'd bottled up a lot of emotion during the past few days.

'I turned down a trip to Belgium at the last minute, but when I got back to the flat, Jim had left on this trip to Paris. Then, I read his name in the list of survivors and I've been sick with worry ever since. I couldn't even get word through to this place,' concluded Jim's wife, her eyes misting with tears.

Helen nodded in the direction of the lifeboat station.

'Jim went for a walk.'

Jim's wife turned eagerly, and saw her husband, leaning on the rails along the sea front, staring at the sea.

Forgetting to thank Helen, she trotted up to Jim. Helen watched for a moment. She saw the coldness on Jim's face. The earnestness on his wife's appealing features. Then they stopped trying to talk at once. Jim smiled. They held hands. His wife kissed him.

Helen set out for the High Street. Suddenly, everything was alright again, in fact, better than it had been before the blizzards.

Only one problem remained. What on earth could she buy Steve for Christmas!

We do hope that you have enjoyed reading this large print book.

Did you know that all of our titles are available for purchase?

We publish a wide range of high quality large print books including:
Romances, Mysteries, Classics
General Fiction
Non Fiction and Westerns

Special interest titles available in large print are:
The Little Oxford Dictionary
Music Book, Song Book
Hymn Book, Service Book

Also available from us courtesy of Oxford University Press:
Young Readers' Dictionary
(large print edition)
Young Readers' Thesaurus
(large print edition)

For further information or a free brochure, please contact us at:
Ulverscroft Large Print Books Ltd.,
The Green, Bradgate Road, Anstey,
Leicester, LE7 7FU, England.
Tel: (00 44) **0116 236 4325**
Fax: (00 44) **0116 234 0205**

THE ECHOING BELLS

Lillie Holland

In Germany Marnie Burness accepts the post of governess at Schloss Beissel. Her charge is Count von Oldenburg's daughter, Charlotte. Despite finding much to disapprove of at the Schloss, against her own principles she falls in love with the Count. Then, when Maria, the Count's wife, is murdered Marnie suspects his involvement. She leaves the Schloss, but will she ever learn the truth about the death of the countess — and will her suspicions of the Count be proved right?